MEN OF HONOR

NEW YORK *TIMES* BESTSELLING AUTHOR

STEPHANIE TYLER

WRITING AS

SE JAKES

MEN OF HONOR, BOOK 3

Can two men let go of the past in order to find their future together?

When helo pilot Glen Rhodes flies Navy SEALS into the most dangerous places on earth, he has nerves of steel. Since his trusted Dom's death three years ago, though, the thought of submitting makes him panic.

Determined to move on and long past ready to release the adrenaline rush from his job, Glen returns to home ground—and to the bar he hasn't had the heart to enter for three long years. There, he meets a man who seems to fit naturally into the void.

Derek Mann has suffered his own losses, and he isn't looking for permanent. Easy conquests don't interest him, either. One look at Glen's proud military bearing and sad eyes tells him that he has a challenge on his hands. And that winning Glen's trust will unleash something wild and beautiful.

The plan is to tread lightly. But from the first touch of skin on skin, there's no holding back…except when it comes to their deepest emotions. A Christmas Eve crisis pushes them both to their limits, leaving them no choice but to let go of the past…or let it pull them apart.

Warning: Contains rough language, rougher sex and warriors who fall hard for one another.

For the readers, who
make me smile daily
with their emails
and support.

1

Glen Rhodes remembered the first time he'd snuck into the leather bar. He'd been seventeen with a good fake ID, and he'd fought with the first man he'd encountered. Hadn't expected to be grabbed and treated like he was there for the taking.

Hadn't understood he'd been in way over his head. If it hadn't been for John…

John was big and broad, a bear in every sense of the word, but Glen hadn't been looking for a bear, just a man to help him deal with his submissive needs.

It had been confusing as hell, and John had helped him make sense out of his wants. Until then, Glen's life consisted of competitive swimming and little else, to the point where he'd started to feel closed in. Constricted.

The panic attacks that began that year had made everything worse. He'd talked to coaches and shrinks, but nothing they recommended helped defuse the frustration. The road to the Olympics was a long one, filled with days and nights of constant practice. Physical stamina was a must, but mental toughness was a necessity—the other half of the puzzle.

It wasn't until he stumbled on BDSM porn one night that he realized what he might be missing. It turned him on like nothing else had.

How to go about getting it was a different story. Fantasy took him only so far, and even though he wasn't hiding his sexuality, there weren't any seventeen- year-old boys he knew who were willing—or able—to tie him up the way he needed.

John gave him that outlet.

John took him home, tied him to the headboard and let him come. And then he'd left him tied for hours and took Glen in ways he'd only seen or read about.

"Virgin," John had murmured, and it hadn't been a problem for him at all.

From that point on, John gave him what he needed without Glen having to do much more than show up. Other types of submission were not for him—he liked spankings but not whips or punishments—he'd urged John to try both with him a few times but it ended in disaster because Glen simply couldn't get off.

Rope bondage or cuffs or spreader bars—Jesus, sometimes just seeing a ball of twine got him hard. And the submission with John focused Glen on his swimming, to the point where he had an amazing Olympic career in front of him if things continued along that vein.

They hadn't. And while he and John were never exclusive, John had always been there for him. His touchstone. He'd assumed, in that naïve way you had when you were young that you and everyone around you would live forever.

Now, a little over ten years later, the bar looked the same. He'd been back here a few times since John's death five years ago, trying a new Dom less than a year after John died.

Too soon. Wrong Dom. Since then, nothing had seemed right, and he just kept one foot in front of the other, did his job and fucked as many men as he could.

Since then, he hadn't let anyone else in—literally, figuratively—and he wasn't sure why he'd turned the car in this direction tonight, why he stood outside, listening to the music and the laughter. It wasn't even Thanksgiving yet, and the lights blinked along the windows, wreath hung on the door… Glen wouldn't be able to escape the time of year.

Christmas always hit Glen hard. John had died in the weeks prior, and although some said Glen should've moved on by now, he hadn't been able to.

But lately, the numbness had been replaced by a deep ache he couldn't fill, no matter how often he fucked random guys.

It was time to allow himself to be tied up again. Whether or not he would find the right Dom remained to be seen. But he'd start at the club he'd met John in, because they knew him. They'd protect him, although he felt stupid for even thinking he'd need that.

You're vulnerable—you need it, his friend Clint, aka Tomcat, had told him the week before. He'd met Clint years earlier, through John's work. John had been with the CIA, although Glen doubted anyone in the Dom/sub world who knew the man would know that. And although Glen rarely saw Clint, they spoke often, with Clint checking up on him at least every couple of months.

And so, because of Clint's words, Glen swallowed his pride and went toward the comfort of the old club, where there were rules and regulations, and not everyone who said they were a Dom was allowed through the door.

He'd promised he wouldn't do anything dumb but damn, he wanted to be fucked stupid—and soon.

A shiver brushed the back of Derek's neck seconds before he spotted the blond walk through the door.

The boy was beautiful—handsome, maybe mid-to-late twenties. The tattoos that ran up and down his arms were a promise of many more under the black wife-beater that he revealed when the black leather jacket slipped off.

He turned to the older Dom, James, sitting next to him at the bar. "Who's that?"

"That's Glen," James said with a half-smile. He'd been watching the boy as well. "I didn't think we'd ever see him here again."

Derek's gut tugged—usually that meant the boy was a pain in the ass or not a good sub at all. But typically, this bar wouldn't allow someone like that inside. "Why not?"

James pointed to the wall and Derek turned his head toward the picture of John.

"He was John's?" John was a legend at this place—part-owner, friend to all. A Dom who taught others what the term really meant. He'd also been retired CIA, although Derek was only privy to that because of his own time in the military.

"For five years, until John died. After that…" James shook his head. "He's never taken another Dom?"

"He tried. But it didn't work. John was a hard memory to live up to." "Maybe he tried someplace else?"

"No way—this is Glen's home. He knows that. John wouldn't have wanted him to go someplace he wasn't known to sub. He's been fucking around in other bars, literally, but that's about it." James looked at Derek. "If he's back here, that means he's looking."

"Any advice?" Because Derek was chomping at the bit to approach him. The shiver touched his neck again and he rubbed the skin there and wondered why this boy hit him so hard.

James fixed him with a hard gaze. "He's not easy. Never was, never will be. He doesn't want the traditional relationship. But if he respects you, the submission you get…"

James didn't finish but Derek knew—could tell by the strut the boy had, even with the sadness in his eyes—that Glen submitting would be a wild and beautiful thing. He'd had that once, a long time ago, and some said he'd been purposely picking the wrong boys since.

They were probably right.

A widowed Dom and a widowed sub typically didn't mix well—both had expectations that were impossible to meet. But he was being tugged in Glen's direction by something, and he glanced at the picture of John and back to Glen.

He watched the other men come up to the boy, hug him, welcome him as he drank his beer slowly. Glen looked overwhelmed after about fifteen minutes, was having trouble making eye contact with people, had his hands stuffed in his pockets, and Derek could see they were fisted. He couldn't think of a better time to make his introduction.

He came up behind the boy and put a hand on the back of his neck, his palm tingling with the contact of the warm skin. Glen stilled immediately and Derek murmured, "Come on—you're about to lose it."

Glen didn't fight, turned and walked next to Derek, not meeting his eyes, walking with his head down. Derek kept up the light rub on his hot skin until they moved to a more private area, ignoring the whispers that started immediately.

"Face the wall," Derek told him.

"I don't do that punishment shit," Glen growled, tried to break away but Derek held him in place, inhaling the boy's scent—beach and cinnamon and that pure scent of a man aroused.

"It's not a punishment. You're on sensory overload, headed to a panic attack.

Now stay. Breathe."

Glen gave a short nod, a flash of appreciation in his dark blue eyes, and did just that. Hung his head, stuffed his hands in his pockets again, and the men remained silent for a few minutes until Glen's breathing became slow and steady. Derek studied his profile—his bearing was military, straight and sure, even with his head down with the kind of perfect posture of a sub. Derek had an urge to kiss him, but that would only end in disaster at the moment.

"Thanks," Glen said finally, lifted his head and looked Derek in the eye. Half challenge, but there was also something else there…uncertainty. Lust, too.

It was enough. "I'm Derek Mann. Come sit. Have a drink."

Glen nodded, sat next to Derek on the couch but asked for a soda when the waiter came to take their order. The waiter obviously recognized Glen, nodded at him, and Glen nodded back and drank half the Coke on his first pull. "I guess you know who I am."

"I know who your Dom was," Derek said. "That's not the same thing at all."

Glen frowned a little, as if he'd never considered that. "You're the only one who had the balls to approach me like that." That obviously sat well with Glen— with Derek too.

"Are you here to play?"

Glen stared at him, the dark blue eyes holding more pain than should be allowed for a young man. "I'm here to get fucked," he said bluntly. "After that…"

Derek let the corner of his mouth tug up. Glen would

be a challenge, as promised. Broken wasn't a word in his vocabulary. "You're military."

"Navy pilot." "Before that?"

"I was headed to the Olympics. Swimming." "What happened?"

The challenge was back in his eyes. "John died and I gave up on everything. I figured if I could do something dangerous, I'd die sooner and then not break my promise to John."

"Which was?" Derek had no right to ask, but he did.

Glen looked right into his eyes, his answer unapologetic. "Not to kill myself after he died."

Why he told the dark-haired Dom that partial lie—since he'd already been in the military when John died—Glen wasn't sure.

Bullshit you're not sure—you want to scare him away.

But the Dom—with the dark brown eyes and chiseled cheekbones and lips that made Glen lick his involuntarily— didn't seem shocked. Sad, maybe, but without the typical pity shit, which Glen had no use for.

Derek was big—broad, muscular—wore his leathers well. His chest and face were smooth—the total opposite of John in every way and it still made Glen hot.

Glen wasn't small but next to this guy…

A flash of fantasy—of being pinned under the Dom,

helpless. Being filled until he didn't think he could take any more. Surrendering.

Damn, it had been so long for him. Fucking guys wasn't giving him anything close to what he needed, and it had taken a trip in here and Derek's touch to make him admit it to himself.

He swore he heard John whispering to him, but he couldn't make out the words.

John. And that made him think of Mark and how bad that scene was, even though the man was as handsome as Derek.

"This was a mistake." He made a move to stand, but Derek held him firmly by the wrist, looked him in the eye and Glen swore the man was hypnotizing him somehow.

"You're looking for a fuck. I'm willing to give you what you need—where's the mistake in that?" Derek asked calmly. "That's not rhetorical, by the way. I expect an answer."

"I can't...not here." He couldn't go into the back rooms, with all the memories. Everything was welling up and his breath was coming fast again and the smells of beer and sex and cologne were stifling him.

"Your place." Derek stood and Glen found himself doing so automatically as well, mainly because Derek still held his wrist. He let go so Glen could put his jacket on and then Derek's hand went on the back of his neck again, leading him through the bar and into the parking lot. "Don't make eye contact with anyone."

Glen didn't argue—Derek was telling him for his own

good. And once he hit the uncrowded space, he took a big lungful of air and glanced toward Derek.

The man hadn't taken his eyes off him. Glen felt…taken care of. Owned. His body missed that feeling.

So much so, he was willing to throw himself at the first guy who showed him attention.

But that wasn't really true.

Derek's voice broke through his reverie. "Did you drive?" Glen pointed to the old Porsche.

"Beautiful baby," Derek whispered as he steered them in its direction, and Glen had the feeling the man wasn't talking only about the car. "Drive me in it."

An order…a request, and it really didn't matter. Glen would take him home. The men in the club wouldn't have let him leave with Derek if the man hadn't been sane, safe, consensual, no matter if Glen met their eyes or not.

Derek stretched his legs as far as he could in the low machine—the seats were all the way back—and the Dom leaned back and closed his eyes as Glen rumbled out of the lot and headed to the highway.

His townhouse was half an hour from the club—he lived close to the base but not on it, because he needed that cushion of privacy, since *don't ask, don't tell* was still very much a reality, repeal or not. Besides, his private life had never been anyone's business. The Navy got its time and Glen got his, and that was the end of it.

He looked over quickly at Derek, whose eyes were still

closed, his big body relaxed, but his cock definitely hard. Glen's own had been that way since Derek touched him. He could still feel the man's hand on his neck even though he'd let go fifteen minutes ago.

How was this man getting home from his place? Where did he even live?

Glen found himself driving more carefully than normal, as if wanting to keep Derek from being jostled. He finally pulled into his driveway and then the garage, letting the door close behind him.

Derek got out immediately, and Glen found the man opening the driver's- side door and helping him out. And Glen fucking blushed at that.

Derek most definitely noticed, gave a little twist of a grin, and Glen felt himself blush harder as he got out of the car and let Derek lead him toward his own house.

"It's okay," Derek murmured and somehow, with the Dom saying that, it was. At least for the moment. What happened once the door opened and Glen let him in, he wasn't sure at all.

2

Glen's place was done in browns and beiges and blues—clean and calming, with comfortable-looking furniture and a modern kitchen that looked like it was barely used.

With red still staining his cheeks, Glen locked the door behind them and pressed buttons on the buzzing alarms.

"Can I get you anything?" Glen asked as he toed his shoes off. "Water would be fine."

Glen grabbed a bottle from the fridge, took the time to pour it in a glass with ice, and Derek couldn't tell if it was manners or the man stalling or a combination. When Glen handed it to him, Derek took a sip and then asked, "What do you need from me, Glen?"

The boy shot him a look, the surprise obvious, and that was good. He was up to this.

"I, ah…fuck." Glen pressed a palm to his forehead. "I don't know. I like to be tied down. Hard. But—"

It was too soon—Derek would need to earn that trust. Coming into the club tonight had drained Glen, and it was up to Derek to make sure he didn't fall apart sooner than he was ready to. "Why don't you let me decide?"

"What if I can't do what you want?"

"It won't be more than you can take. It won't be a scene. You'll get what you need."

It took a few minutes for him to nod yes. Derek sat in one of the leather chairs, glass in hand. "Strip for me."

Glen barely hesitated, then stripped his shirt and his jeans, a defiant look in his eyes.

He wouldn't go down on his knees into position—and Derek wasn't going to make him. Not to prove a point, anyway. Instead, he took the time to appreciate Glen's sculpted, lean body, the thick, jutting cock belying any protests the boy might make. He spread his own legs and let Glen's eyes roam his body—there was no missing the swell of his cock through his pants, despite the tight leather. "Like what you see?"

Glen nodded slowly, began to stroke himself without breaking Derek's gaze. Derek finished his water, put the glass down and walked to the boy, not telling him to stop his stroking.

"Beautiful." He ran a hand over the tattoos that covered him, not surprised when Glen reached out with his free hand and pulled him in for a kiss. Glen's hand wound in his hair, holding him closer, definitely taking charge, and Derek allowed it, because the boy knew how to kiss. Glen tasted like heat and sin. And then Derek changed the rhythm when he put his hand on the back of Glen's neck and began fucking his mouth with his tongue, taking back all the control, and Glen opened his mouth wider, acquiescing.

Glen would enjoy submitting far more than he was willing to admit. The boy would have to have nerves of steel to fly combat missions—it took equal strength to submit. Glen was a tough-ass son of a bitch. Just what Derek wanted, someone to push back, to challenge him. He wanted that spark, the fight, which made working for the submission that much more satisfying.

When Derek pulled back, he asked, "You want to keep trying to scare me away by being defiant or are you going to let me take over now and fuck that tight ass any way I want to?"

Glen drew in a stuttered breath and his body trembled. "I haven't…submitted—or bottomed—in a long time."

"Since John?"

"A year after John died, I tried but…" He was holding it together well but he seemed horrified at the small amount of emotion he was showing. "I don't know why I'm telling you all this."

"Because you need to." Derek stroked his biceps, still tasting the man on his tongue. "Show me where your bed is."

Glen did, and Derek followed him into the bedroom with the king-sized bed covered in a gray comforter and a headboard definitely meant for tying someone up to.

Derek could give Glen the same effect just as well with a command. He pushed the younger man into bed after pulling the covers down, and Glen sat against the pillows, looking uncertain.

Derek stripped his own shirt and knelt between Glen's legs. The boy looked confused when Derek stroked him and then licked a path along his abs and inner thighs.

"Derek?"

"Yes, Glen." "I thought…"

"Don't think." With that, he took Glen's cock deep in his mouth, sucking hard, loving the way the boy's body arched in surprise.

Derek's mouth was hot and wet, sucking him in while Glen watched.

There was never any doubt during the entire experience that Derek was in charge.

All he had to do was let Glen's cock slip from his mouth and say, "Raise your arms above your head and don't move them until I tell you that you can."

Glen complied. It was a small step back that left him wanting for more, which was surely part of Derek's plan. And then Derek began playing with his cock, his balls, spread Glen's legs where he wanted them, with the unspoken command that Glen was to leave them where Derek positioned them.

"You must look beautiful all tied up," Derek said finally. "The things I'd do to you…"

"What?" Glen gasped out, because Derek was pressing a

finger along his perineum while stroking his cock.

"Don't come," Derek warned, and God, that would be hard as hell, but he could do it. "I'd tie you so tightly you couldn't move. I'd use nipple clamps on you, because you love them. Don't you, beautiful baby?"

He did. Nodded and closed his eyes for a second, because just looking at the handsome man waiting calmly between his legs could take him over the edge.

"I know you want to be fucked tonight…but you're not in charge here. I think you've already accepted that."

"Please," he heard himself whimper, knew that wasn't always permitted, but there was encouragement in Derek's eyes. He wanted more, wanted to know how Glen was feeling, and Glen let him know in no uncertain terms when Derek stroked his cock, long, hard strokes, just the way he liked it. Heard himself yelling his head off, because screw his inhibitions and his neighbors.

Getting his cock sucked was an unexpected turn of events and he was reveling in it.

Derek was spreading him, then fingering his ass while using his tongue to delve into Glen's piss slit, which made him jump practically to the goddamned ceiling. Only Derek's strong arms kept him in place firmly on the mattress and Glen allowed himself to close his eyes and get lost in the sensations. When Derek told him to come, Glen didn't hesitate, the orgasm long and drawn-out and so goddamned satisfying.

You're perfectly safe.

Maybe Derek even murmured that to him. It wouldn't be the first time a Dom since John had, but Glen finally believed it.

But he was so drained and sleepy, wondered what Derek would do next.

Steeled himself for it, even.

The man simply pulled Glen to his chest and said, "Sleep."

And for the first time in a long time in bed, Glen did as he was told.

3

What Glen had needed was a blowjob and sleep, which was what he got. When he woke, he was alone and he wondered if it was a dream. Why the Dom didn't demand more. And how he'd gotten home, because Glen should've at least been the one to call him a cab.

Glen wanted to think less of the man for it but knew he couldn't. John hadn't held back their first nights together because he'd known that was what Glen had needed. Derek had held back for the same reason. He'd had Glen's submission last night, even thought Glen hadn't thought himself ready or willing to give it.

He stared at the ceiling, knowing the day would pass too damned slowly for him. He'd go back to the club tonight, his last night of leave for a while, because after that he needed to be mission ready. The SEAL team he flew was hunkered down on base and preparing. He would join in, along with his copilot, once they had their shit together.

He'd train the way they did. In order to back them up, he'd come up with several different plans if things went to shit.

26

SE JAKES

Which they always seemed to do at the last minute. But Glen was good at his job—he'd run the scenarios a million different ways until he was satisfied he could get all the men out safely.

But tonight was all his.

His cell vibrated. *Clint.* The man had known Glen had plans to go to the bar last night, and he was no doubt checking up.

"How'd it go? Did you get laid?" Clint asked. "Jesus, Clint."

"What? Isn't that what you were looking for?" "Maybe."

"Give me his name."

"I'm not letting you run a sheet on him." "Yeah, you are."

He gave the name, then said, "I'm thinking former military. If I had to guess, Marine."

"Guy's a Marine," Clint confirmed. "So you know him."

"I've never fucked him, if that's what you're asking."

"You're both Doms, so I pretty much assumed that," Glen said. "You want details, don't you?"

"Why do you make me pull everything out of you?" Glen had no doubt Clint had already gotten information on Derek.

"More fun that way," Clint said with a laugh, and his next words confirmed Glen's suspicions that Clint had checked up on Derek already. "Okay, here's what my buddy told me about him."

Clint launched into a few things Derek was into, nothing out of the ordinary, but Glen tucked away several pieces of information that could be very helpful in the future when he wanted to please his Dom.

His Dom. Your Dom. He felt a little dizzy at those words.

"Hey, you still there?" Clint asked.

"Yeah. Just a little…freaked out." "Guess you like him, then." "Maybe."

"If he hurts you, I'll kill him."

Clint's wasn't an empty promise. Glen muttered something about overbearing CIA guys and said, "Gotta run."

He meant it literally. Had to get the energy out so he wouldn't be a mess.

Clint just snorted and told him to keep in touch before he hung up.

A long run, a longer shower, complete with jacking off helped to take a little of the edge off, but it wasn't enough. Derek probably expected him to be nervous, but Glen hated being off his game this way.

The Dom hadn't left a number or a note, but the care the man had taken with him… It had been a long time since someone cared. And as stupid as it sounded, as fast as it had happened, Glen knew he wasn't wrong.

Now he just had to decide how far he was going to let things go, how ready he was to really let someone else in beyond a quick fuck.

"How'd it go?" James asked when Derek settled in next to him at the bar and ordered a beer on tap.

"If he comes back, I guess it went well." Derek ran a hand

through his hair and played with the beer glass instead of actually drinking. Sounded calmer than he felt. "He and John must've been something together."

"They never did public scenes but yeah, they were good for each other," James acknowledged. "John had a few different subs, but he was closest with Glen. Even when the boy enlisted, they stayed together."

Derek tucked than information away, since it differed slightly from what Glen had told him.

James continued, "Big age difference, though. Glen was twenty-two when John died. John was forty-seven when the emphysema killed him."

Derek was thirty-seven. He'd never liked the young ones. Glen was a perfect age. A perfect fuck. And so much more…

Which meant the whole damned thing would blow up in his face. "He tried once before, you know," James said. "With Mark."

Derek was familiar with Mark. The man used pain for pain's sake, liked his whips and blood play, and God, that must've been a massive miscalculation on Glen's part. Because, although the boy had a wild streak a mile wide, he didn't need to be beaten in order to be tamed. Just the opposite—he needed gentling.

Derek had recognized it immediately. Glen would bolt if ridden too hard right now. He needed complete safety— that's what he got off on. From there, it would be one of the wildest rides ever.

"I don't think I've ever seen you nervous." James tapped Derek's beer and Derek downed half of it.

"That obvious?"

"Probably only to me." James smiled, and then nodded toward the front door.

His heart beating wildly, Derek watched Glen walk in, the same thing happening as last night, with men greeting him, although several of the Doms glanced back toward Derek to see what he'd do.

Glen looked, too, and Derek motioned for the boy to come to him, suddenly feeling way more settled than he had minutes before, especially because of Glen's small smile, meant only for him.

"Nice job." James gave him a clap on the shoulder as Glen walked toward them. Went to Derek and nodded and then turned and did the same to James, before the man hugged him.

"Didn't get to talk to you last night," James said. "You're looking good."

"Thanks."

"I hope this means you're not going to be a stranger anymore."

Glen flicked a glance at Derek. A shy smile that couldn't have been any more effective if the boy crawled directly inside his fucking heart, and he was done. "I think you'll see me around."

"Come on." Derek slid off the stool and brought Glen

to the back, found an empty couch in a quiet corner. For a while, the men simply talked. Sports. Pop culture. Navy life.

"I was a Marine," Derek said finally.

"Like I couldn't tell," Glen muttered, although he had a smile on his face. And yes, Derek still did have the countenance of a military man, but he knew Glen had done some checking on him as well.

"Want me to take you over my knee right here?" Derek's words came out as more of a growl than he intended, but Glen drew in a sharp breath and his cock hardened in the soft cotton of his jeans. "I'll keep that in mind. For later."

Glen nodded, his eyes bright. "About what happened… last night…" "Problem?"

"No." The boy shifted. "I didn't mean to disappoint you."

"If you had, I wouldn't have called you over. I wouldn't have tucked you in and let you drool on my shoulder until dawn."

"I don't drool."

"No, you don't." He looked at the boy. "I was hoping you'd come back tonight. That's why I'm here—for you."

"Me too."

"Do you have to work tomorrow?" "I have weekend leave."

"My house, then." Derek began walking, giving Glen no choice but to follow. "Is your car here?"

"Yeah."

"I'll follow you—drop it off and we'll have dinner first."

Pride flooded Glen when he realized Derek had been waiting for him. He watched the Dom stride through the back exit, stared at his wide shoulders and back, and as his gaze dropped lower, Derek turned suddenly.

"Like what you see?"

Glen nodded, and Derek shook his head and continued walking, pointed to his truck. Glen got into his car to follow, had to force himself to concentrate on the road and Derek's taillights, because his mind was racing. He wanted this—wanted Derek—but he had his own set of rules.

What if Derek didn't want to hear them? Or worse, deal with them?

Finally, he pulled into his garage. Got out and closed the door behind him and took a deep breath before getting into the passenger's side of Derek's truck. Sat and stared straight ahead, and finally realized that Derek wasn't pulling out.

If Derek wanted to know his bottom line, better to tell him now. If he didn't want to stick around after that, so be it.

Damn, he wanted Derek to stick around, though.

Before he could stop himself, he told the Dom, "I like being a submissive. I don't like rules and regs, all that master shit. I give myself to you not only because I want to, but because you deserve it. I want the pleasure. I want to be tied up. I'm not into any of that *sit in a corner because you were bad* shit. And I can't stay tied up all night, sleep on floors, wear collars or be ordered all night, because I have a job flying Navy helos and if I'm not alert, people die." It all came out in a big breath and he shifted, his body tight from the confession.

He hadn't looked at Derek at all while he'd spoken, not because of any D/s rules, but because he didn't want to see disapproval. But Derek's hand cupped his chin and tugged until Glen did look him in the eye.

He saw exactly what he'd hoped to in Derek's gaze. "That all works for me. I'm not looking for a traditional sub. Just someone who likes to let me do what I do best, which is dominate."

"I just…needed you to know my bottom line. Because you don't know me and—"

Derek interrupted him, his tone firm but gentle. "You have nothing to prove to me, boy. If you were John's, you're special. But I knew that about you from the second you walked into the club."

He released Glen's chin, touched his lips with his thumb, tracing the bottom one until Glen felt himself harden.

"You don't trust me fully yet," he continued and Glen nodded. "I wouldn't expect you to."

"Why not?"

"You've been hanging around with the wrong people if you have to ask that."

"John wasn't wrong." Glen heard the defensiveness in his own tone and wondered what that was all about.

"No, but you were young. You should know better now.

This isn't about one night of play. This is about building something between us. At least that's what I'm looking for."

"It…I don't…" Fuck. He hadn't expected anything like this. But it sounded like he should be expecting a lot more for himself. "Me too."

Derek smiled. "Good. Let's grab some dinner and we can talk more."

As he pulled out into the street, Glen wondered if it could really be this easy.

He didn't know if it was supposed to be.

Certain things had been. When the world was too much, he'd head over to John's and let him work his magic. There were no questions asked. No negotiation. John would do whatever he wanted and Glen would tell himself that's what he wanted.

At the time, it might've been. But now, his life—everything about him—had changed. He supposed it was time for the rules to change as well.

Derek picked a Chinese restaurant close to his house. They ordered Yuengling beers and dishes to share, and Derek settled back against the rounded, private booth and put his feet on either side of Glen's under the table in an obvious show of possessiveness. Thought about grabbing the boy and kissing the shit out of him, but hell, he wouldn't do that to anyone with an active-duty military career.

As if Glen knew what he was thinking, he shook his head and bit his bottom lip.

"I'll do that for you later myself," Derek told him.

As they settled into dinner, Derek knew he needed to move past the lighter topics they'd discussed earlier back at the bar. They'd covered some good ground in the car—Derek was more than pleased to see Glen looking out for himself, stating his wants and needs. But there were still more questions to be asked. "Are you still suicidal?"

Glen worked his chopsticks around a piece of chicken and looked Derek right in the eyes before answering, "Anyone who flies military choppers has a death wish, but you knew that already."

Derek had his answers—the boy liked danger and adrenaline, but mentally, he was stable. He wouldn't have been able to fool the military docs all these years. "I didn't think they'd let you in with all those tats."

"If you're good enough, they'll let you do anything," Glen said. "I cover them."

Derek wanted him naked for long enough to go over all of them—with his lips, tongue, fingertips. "You gave up swimming long before John died."

"Yes," he admitted. "Just wanted to see how serious you were." "I guess I passed your test."

Glen just gave a half grin at that. "Did you know John?"

"By his reputation, mostly. I met him a few times in passing, but I was active duty then so I wasn't frequenting the bar much." Derek pushed the remaining food toward Glen—the boy would need to keep up his reserves for the job he did. He probably still had the appetite of a teenager and worked out enough to be able to eat a great deal of calories per day.

Glen predictably gave no argument, finished the food and settled back in obvious contentment. "That's good. I didn't eat much today."

"Why not?"

He gave a sheepish shrug and Derek knew the answer— the same case of nerves that had kept Derek himself on edge all day as well. So he let Glen off the hook with that one, but continued, "I'm guessing you met John at the bar."

"Yeah. I snuck in there one night with a fake ID. Had no clue what I was doing. Everything happened the way it did last night—all these guys came up to me and I thought I was going to lose it. I was just about to turn and leave when John took my arm and brought me to the bar. Sat me down and asked my real age."

"You were nowhere near twenty-one, I'm guessing."

"Seventeen. I was with John from seventeen," he said. "No one knew that. I told him I had no idea what I was doing— Christ, I was a total fucking innocent, and he had every right to turn me away and let me find the trouble I'd gone in looking for. But he took me on instead."

"From what I knew of him, he didn't like the young ones."

"No, he didn't. But he liked me." Glen's face glowed with pride.

"I can see why." He tried to picture Glen on that first night, young and scared and still willing to try anything. And then he realized with a start that, even though John wasn't around any longer, he still didn't want to picture this boy—his boy—with anyone but him. Where that sudden surge came from he had no clue, but it startled him. Must've shown on his face, because Glen asked, "You all right, Derek?"

"Just having a hard time picturing you with anyone but me," he said honestly. "But I'm okay with you talking about it. I think you have to."

Glen nodded. "I never really have, with anyone. Kept a lot in, with good reason. It's private stuff."

"You said you tried subbing with someone else after him."

Glen's face hardened, almost imperceptibly. His hand tightened around the beer and he took a long drink before nodding yes. Then said, "It was a year after John died. I thought I was ready."

"Too soon."

"It wasn't too soon. He was the wrong guy. You have no idea how wrong." "Did he hurt you?"

"Are you a one-man rescue machine?" Glen demanded.

The boy would bend for him. How Glen would look, tied, arms and legs, helpless, had make Derek jack off twice in the shower.

If the look of complete pleasure at his orgasm last night plus his submissive compliance was any indication, Derek knew he was correct.

"Isn't that what you want?" Derek asked calmly, partially enjoying the confusion on Glen's face. "Boy, you've got a mouth on you. Between that and your earlier Marine comment, I'm thinking you really want me to take you in hand."

Glen opened his mouth but a soft huff came out instead of words. If Derek reached for his crotch, he was certain he'd find Glen hard as hell. He passed his keys across the table. "Go start the truck—I'll be out after I pay. And no more mouth from you."

Glen bit his bottom lip and waited for a long moment before he moved out of the booth, shoved his hands in his pockets, and Derek forced himself not to smile at the boy's discomfort.

He took his time paying the bill, hit the head, then ambled out into the nice, warm car. Didn't say anything more than a few directions until they got to the woods behind his house. All his property. No one would bother him on his own land, but Glen wouldn't know that.

When Glen parked, Derek told him, "Get in the back."

He'd already put the second row of seats down to give them more room, had done so before he'd driven to the bar just in case.

Glen gave him a hesitant glance before gracefully getting

into the back. "Clothes off. On your hands and knees, facing the back. Spread your legs."

He watched in the rearview mirror to see Glen doing as he asked. Only then did he join him. Rubbed a hand over the boy's back and down over his ass. "Nice."

He leaned forward and bound Glen's wrists with leather straps that were soft on the inside and would leave no marks, and then chained them hard to the latch so Glen couldn't move them at all. Forced into position with no out, Glen groaned when he realized it.

The sound shot through Derek more effectively than a hand on his cock. His beautiful boy, tied, all for his pleasure.

He ran his tongue down the boy's spine, starting at his neck and ending at the crack of his ass. Stopped short of breaching where they both wanted him to go, heard the grunt of frustration as he worked his body over Glen's.

"Hope the cops don't come through to find you like this," he whispered as he ground his jean-clad cock against Glen's bare ass, the fabric touching the sensitive hole. "All spread, giving yourself to me. What would you tell them— that this is exactly what you want?"

Glen nodded.

"Tell me," he demanded. "It's what I want." "Because you were bad?" "Yes, very."

"On purpose."

"Yes." A hard swallow. "I wanted this. Please." "Then don't move."

The boy's body was tensed up from so many different emotions, the least of which was sexual need. This was about being tied, the anticipation, and Derek drew it out by taking off his shirt and unzipping his jeans slowly. Put a condom on and grabbed some lube from the front seat. Watched Glen try to steady his body as his cock hung in the air, no doubt wanting any kind of friction and finding none.

When Glen finally stilled, he slapped Glen's ass twice—hard slaps to each cheek—and heard the low gasp of pleasure. A third and fourth rang through the air and Glen cursed and received two more, even as Derek kept a firm hand on the boy's lower back.

He moved to top Glen, so his cock rubbed along the seam of Glen's ass, brushed his hole with the promise of the fucking he was about to get.

"I can do anything I want to you," Derek whispered, ran a hand in Glen's hair. "Little boy would like that, wouldn't he?"

"Yeah." Glen's voice was husky, heavy with every wish he held.

"Spread your legs farther," Derek ordered, and Glen complied. He spread some lube on his fingers and his cock, worked one then two inside Glen while still remaining mostly on top of him. Moved them in and out, brushing his prostate a couple of times—loving the responses he was getting. "I want you ready for me. Begging for it."

"Please." It was more a growl than a plea, a demand that couldn't be ignored. The space was small with their two bodies—and between his covering Glen's and the fact that his wrists were tied, he was giving Glen the experience of being totally immobile. He pushed inside, heard Glen's sharp intake of breath.

"You're big…so goddamned big," he said finally when Derek was halfway inside.

"And I'm not stopping. You don't want me to."

"God, yes, keep going," Glen breathed as Derek pushed the rest of the way in until he was buried up to his balls inside the boy. Glen was so damned tight and hot, his ass contracting around Derek's cock, milking him without Derek even having to move. But Glen wanted him to move, pushed back into his cock as much as he could and murmured, "Derek…"

It was part plea, part prayer, and with that, Derek pinned him down hard and took him fast. Glen, having no quarter or choice in how he was being claimed, simply put his head down and let himself be ridden the way Derek wanted to.

"Don't you come yet," he told Glen as he slammed his prostate repeatedly, watched the tension in Glen's back begin to dissipate just from the way he was being held.

"Touch my cock—I need that," he begged in a raw voice and Derek did as he asked since he was taking so much, trusting so well. Stroked the boy's hard member in tandem with the fucking until he felt his balls tighten and knew he couldn't hang on much longer.

"Come now—right goddamned now," he told Glen, who shot his load all over Derek's hand. In turn, Derek pumped his load inside of Glen, filling the condom. Wishing he didn't have to pull out, wanting to remain in place as long as possible. Finally, he moved and took the condom off. Wrapped and tossed it into a plastic bag.

He kissed the back of Glen's neck, listened to him breathe until it went from riotous to calm. "In the restaurant, when I said you got involved too soon after John, I wasn't judging you. But a year's grief for what you had wasn't enough— you didn't make a choice based on your needs. You made a choice based on loneliness."

Glen swallowed hard, asked, "How do you know that?"

"Because I did the same thing," he admitted. "We deserve time to heal. We don't always allow it because it's easier to be with someone else than to hurt."

With his head still buried in his arms, Glen said, "I want to know more about that…when you're ready to tell me."

He would share, but not tonight. Instead, he reached forward and undid the cuffs and the lock and helped Glen turn over. The boy would be stiff for a little while, and he rubbed the circulation back into his arms as Glen stared up at him, his stomach covered with come.

"So fucking beautiful," he murmured. "Let me take you back to the house and clean you up."

Although it appeared that Derek was asking him, it was part command. Still, Glen got the feeling he'd be allowed to refuse, because Derek waited for him to nod his consent.

"Stay here. I'll drive us to the house."

Glen complied, mainly because he was too damned content to move. His limbs sang from the bindings, his ass burned and his mind was finally quiet.

The truck crunched over snow and leaves, and out the windows, Glen watched them come out of the woods and felt the car find pavement.

In less than two minutes, they were pulling into a garage. Derek got out and opened the hatch to let Glen out that way, still naked. "We were on my property the whole time. You were always safe. I'll never do anything to interfere with your career."

That warmed Glen more than he already was. He let Derek help him out— the chill inside the garage felt good on his skin, and for a moment, he stood there letting the night air wash over him. Then Derek tugged him inside and brought him upstairs.

The house was sparingly lit, but Glen caught sight of brown leather couches and comfortable surroundings. Upstairs, he was directed to get into the king- sized bed with the metal headboard perfect for binding someone and damn, he was hard again.

"Someone wants to be fucked again, don't they?"

"Yes." God, the one word was a definite plea—he couldn't hide it.

Derek swiped the precome from Glen's cock and used it to wet the head, stroked him until his hips rose and fell on the mattress.

It was good, but he wanted Derek back on top of him, holding him, fucking him until he couldn't see past the pleasure. So he spread his legs and reached up to grip the headboard's rungs, holding on tightly, his muscles straining.

Derek stopped to put on a condom finally. Then he took some soft rope and bound Glen's wrists over his head. One ankle only, because he took Glen's other thigh and bent it so he could really get inside of him deeply.

And he did go deep, entered him in one long stroke, all while holding Glen's leg to optimize the pleasure for Glen. But he kept his thrusts deliberately paced, until Glen wanted to claw the ceiling with frustration. Couldn't do much but lie there and take it, which of course made him harder than ever. "You want it faster?"

"Yes."

"But that's up to me, right? And you like it when I take your control away."

Glen nodded, teeth clenched. Because his wants were fighting one another right now, and he was confused and horny and his skin felt too tight. He was sweating, his body ached for more, and he heard himself whisper, "Fuck me, daddy."

Derek froze for a millisecond and then bucked up into him, hard, groaning as his body responded to those words as if they had an uncontrollable pull. Completely lost it, fucked him until Glen saw stars, cried out Derek's name and came in hot spurts on their stomachs.

And for the first time in a long time—maybe ever—Glen wished his wrists weren't bound, so he could wrap his arms around Derek's shoulders to hold the man while they both came. Wondered what the hell that was all about, even as his body still came down from the high of the orgasm.

Derek remained on top of him, only letting Glen's leg drop. Dammit, his body began to tremble all over from everything that had happened that night, like he was finally letting down all his guards.

When Derek felt his shaking, he immediately undid the bindings and pulled Glen close, holding him tighter than ropes ever could. "Relax—you're safe. Really goddamned safe."

He stoked Glen's hair until all that remained was comfort. And he was comfortable, even knowing this man for less than forty-eight hours. He'd made good on his promises—Glen bore no marks and had had no punishments he hadn't been begging for.

Finally, Derek lifted his head, his cheeks flushed from exertion and asked, "Who told you I liked that?"

Glen smiled and buried his face against his shoulder. Murmured, "I have my sources."

"I like that you asked about me. But you're so getting put over my knee for it. In fact, I think that makes at least two spankings I owe you, because the one in the car didn't count."

It counted for Glen because the slaps had been hard enough that he could still feel them, even on the soft sheets. But he wasn't about to complain, instead traced small circles on the bare skin of Derek's shoulder. "That drove you nuts. Loved watching you lose it like that."

"Bet you did." Derek kept him so close. "I want you to stay tonight. Will you be able to sleep or should I drive you home? I want you safe in the air, and I know that means regular sleep."

Glen looked at him and knew the man did really mean it.

This man got it—and him—and that scared him more than anything. "I think I'll be okay to stay."

"Good." He went to the bathroom and came back with a washcloth to wipe Glen's stomach. "You can shower in the morning. I want you to smell me on you all night."

Glen got hard and figured that if he didn't start gaining some self-control, he'd come whenever Derek started talking.

"Come on." Derek shifted to move the covers and Glen got in next to him. There were no orders but Derek was still in control, and fuck, Glen liked that, liked the way the man ordered him around and made him come.

"Can I ask you something?" he asked, heard the sleep in his own voice but resisted it for a while longer.

"Yes."

"Before, when I told you my…needs…" He paused. "Do you have any?" "Of course."

Glen stopped his mind from racing ahead to what they could possibly be and whether or not he'd be able to comply with them. But Derek put a calming hand on the back of Glen's neck and kissed him for a few minutes, his tongue stroking gently along Glen's.

When he pulled away, he told Glen, "The rules I have aren't for you. They're for me. My rule is to keep you happy."

"Keep me happy?" Glen repeated.

"It's not my responsibility to make you happy. Once you're there, I'll keep you that way." Derek paused. "When we're playing, I don't want you to think you can't stop it. But I like pushing you beyond what you think are your limits. Because I think you need that."

Glen thought so too.

Derek let him sleep the next morning, fucked him twice before they got into the shower. Spent a lazy Sunday together that went much faster than Glen would've liked. They ate. Watched a couple of movies.

When Derek dropped him off at home, they had each other's cell and home numbers. No other promises spoken, but they were there, bonding them already in the short time they'd been together.

Still, he hadn't told Derek he was leaving for a mission in the morning and had no idea when he'd be back. He knew Derek would understand why he had to disappear. But they were still so new… Derek didn't know his patterns.

The man could think Glen had disappeared. And so, on the way to the base on Monday morning, he left Derek a note in his mailbox. No email trail, just a simple drawing of his gold wings that he was pretty sure Derek would understand.

Derek found the drawing of the wings in his box that next afternoon. Fingered it—smiled that the boy cared enough to let him know he was on mission status. Said a few prayers for Glen and threw himself into his work until the boy returned.

5

Glen had been gone for nearly three weeks. The clandestine mission in the mountains of Afghanistan had him doing constant pickups and a lot of waiting around for the SEALs to gather their intel. Osama was dead, but there was still a lot of cleanup in the area to contend with. He was on constant call, sleeping little, flying and firing at the same time. All in all, a successful mission.

When the team returned to the States, they spent days debriefing. Going over every detail to see what they could've changed and why. It was probably one of the most important parts of the job, and when it was over, Glen went home and slept for twenty-four hours straight. Woke to darkness. Eleven at night on a Saturday.

He glanced at his phone, thought about calling Derek but decided he'd rather surprise him instead. Showered, dressed and called a cab in the hopes that Derek would be the one driving him home that night.

He scanned the lot as the cab drove in, exhaled when he saw Derek's truck. He went in through the back, hoping to avoid contact with a lot of the men. Coming back from a mission, he was always twitchy. This time, more so, probably because he wasn't sure how Derek would react to his having been gone for so long.

Of course, the first goddamned person he saw was Mark, the Dom he'd attempted a relationship with the year after John died. A real mistake on a number of levels.

The man was good-looking, but that wasn't enough to make up for the amount of pain he'd leveled at Glen. Although it had all occurred years earlier, his insides still ached at the abuse he'd let happen more than once. They'd only been together for a month, at most, before Glen extricated himself and avoided the club—and this entire scene—until the night he'd met Derek.

"Hey, heard you started coming around again." Mark held out his hand and Glen shook it reluctantly.

He tried to look over Mark's shoulder, but the hallway was dark and he couldn't make out anyone at the bar. "I'm meeting someone," he said, tried to step around Mark, who was obviously not wanting to let him pass.

"Heard you've been with Derek," he said.

Glen attempted to push past him but Mark planted an open palm against his chest. Glen wasn't allowed to fight when not in a combat situation. With his training, hitting someone could have deadly consequences and he took that seriously as hell. So he remained in place to hear whatever bullshit Mark wanted to spew and then he'd leave.

"What's it to you if I have? We're over, in case you can't remember," he told Mark, who grinned that small, mean little smile that made Glen cringe inside. Mainly because he couldn't believe that, at one point in his life, he'd been so goddamned weak.

"You're not his type." "Why's that?"

"Because you're not into pain. You can't handle the whip," Mark told him. "You know his sub died, right? Since then, no one can deal with Derek full-time because he's too rough. His last sub has scars from him on his back. He'll start out slow, like he's following your rules, but then he does exactly what he wants."

"And you're telling me this because…"

"Just looking out for you, baby."

Glen bit back what he wanted to say, allowed the comment to die in his throat the way his hopes for Derek being different did as well.

Trusting Mark had been one of the stupidest things he'd ever done. This whole idea of finding someone new to Dom him was stupid. He couldn't shake the feeling that he should've outgrown this—the need to be tied down.

In the eyes of his parents, being gay was a complete aberration. The rest of it further branded him a sick little boy according to his mother, after he confessed what he'd been doing with John to the psychologist she'd forced him to visit.

He'd nearly been locked up in a psych facility—they'd threatened him with that to within an inch of his life. He'd stopped seeing John for a month.

She'd followed him to John's house one afternoon and confronted them. Although John stood up for him like no one had—both before and after he was kicked out—he knew it wouldn't do any good.

He hadn't seen or spoken to his parents in ten years. They referred to him as sick, tried to bring charges against John for attempting to control their son.

Ultimately, they'd been forced to drop the whole thing, because there was no merit. Beyond that, the scandal would've proved too embarrassing for them. They'd already dealt with more than they could handle.

The Navy had been thrilled to acquire him. The Coast Guard fought for him as well, wanted him to be a rescue swimmer, but Glen refused to make a career out of something that brought him so many bad memories. He'd agreed to fly Navy choppers into combat situations because it was so totally out of his knowledge base and comfort zone, and he'd fucking loved it.

The prospect of sharing all this with Derek made him want to pull the covers over his head and hide, even though he was far from a coward.

But he'd never expected to connect with anyone this quickly. And there was no doubt in his mind that he had.

He caught a flash of Derek coming up from behind Mark—the rest happened in a split second that made Glen watch with pride and trepidation.

"You don't touch him—or talk to him ever again," Derek said, his tone leaving no room for negotiation.

"I just told him the truth about you and your last sub, since you didn't," Mark said. Glen watched Derek get his temper in check, as if deciding Mark wasn't worth it.

"Get out of my face," he told Mark quietly, evenly, his eyes never leaving Glen's face, looking to see if he was hurt or upset.

He wasn't sure what he was.

"Maybe you two deserve each other. You know, Glen just walked out on me—he'll do the same to you," the man sneered. "For the month we were together, I had to keep him tied most of the time to make him submit."

"You bastard." Derek had his hands around the man's throat until Glen touched his shoulder.

"He's not worth it. Derek, don't get into trouble—not for him." "You let your sub tell you what to do?" Mark wheezed.

"He's a man, which is more than you'll ever be." With that, Derek dropped him, and Mark finally walked away.

Derek motioned for Glen to follow him farther toward the back, where it was quiet and private, the place where they'd had their first interaction. Glen's heart raced—he wasn't sure he wanted to follow Derek, because surely there would be a punishment for what he'd done. And Derek knew how he felt about that kind of thing.

But he owed the man an explanation of why he was talking to Mark, at the very least, and so he did. Let Derek manhandle him so his back was pressed to the wall, Derek an immovable force in front of him. And fuck it all if Glen wasn't hard already at the holding and the proximity.

"Why didn't you call me? Let me know you were coming here?" Derek demanded.

"Because I'm a grown goddamned man. I came here to find you." Glen wasn't ready for this challenge, but Mark had pissed him off. Worried him, and he hated the man and himself for it.

"You should've called me before you came in. You should've let me walk you in."

"I'm more than capable—"

"You're freaked out. You just came back from a mission. You're worse than you were the first night I met you." Derek's tone was calm, his eyes flashed with something beyond anger that Glen didn't recognize.

Without warning, Derek reached up and twisted Glen's nipple hard through the T-shirt he wore under his black leather jacket as if his fingers were a clamp. Glen gasped and his cock leaked precome inside his jeans. Derek pressed his hips against Glen's, and Glen was effectively held in goddamned place.

Derek brought his thumbnail to press the tip of the nipple, and Glen jolted. "Not here," Glen said, because they were against the wall by the bathroom.

But Derek didn't listen to him, and there had been no "please" attached to it. He knew what would happen when

Derek let go of his nipple, how the rush of blood would trigger an orgasm.

He was vaguely aware that men walked by. No one could really see much but it didn't matter. Derek was marking him, claiming him as surely as if he were fucking him on the bar in front of all of them.

He got harder at that thought. Stared at Derek and recognized the emotion he'd seen before. Worry.

"You're getting it now?" Derek growled, holding the nipple tighter. "If you're with me in here, I'm in charge—and it's usually for your own good."

Glen nodded, his eyes wide, cock leaking. Held in place by nothing more than fingers pressing his nipple, he was excited at the touch—the power it held.

"Are you going to walk in here without me again?" Derek demanded. "No."

"If Mark approaches you and I'm not around, what are you going to do?" "Walk away. Call you."

Derek twisted harder and Glen rethought his answer. "If we're in here, I won't leave your side so that won't happen."

"Ah, good boy." Derek nodded. "I'm going to let you come in your pants.

Bury your face in my neck when you come and apologize."

Glen nodded and Derek kissed him first, the pressure on his nipple increasing until it tingled from lack of blood flow, with Derek's tongue caressing his mouth like the man had all the time in the world.

Glen tried his best not to squirm, more from salvaging what little pride he had left than anything, because he was obviously turned on as hell, but it was no use. And when Derek let go of his nipple, there was no warning. His body bucked with the orgasm—tried to hold it back but it was impossible to do so. He saw stars and came hard, his cry muffled in Derek's neck.

"Sorry…so fucking sorry," he heard himself groan, felt the tears rise even as the orgasm continued to pound through him.

"I know, beautiful baby…I know." Derek held him tight. "I guess we both have a past."

"I didn't want to believe him," Glen said, his voice tight.

"But you did."

He couldn't blame the boy—it was all so new and Derek had put off talking to him about Jared the last time they'd been together. But he still forced Glen to look at him. His eyes were red rimmed and it broke Derek's heart as he waited for Glen's answer.

"I didn't… I'm…" "Scared."

Glen nodded.

"I would never harm a sub," Derek said evenly. "That wasn't what bothered me."

"What did he tell you?"

"He said…you like it rough. And that you start light but then…" Glen shook his head.

"Did I push you too hard the last time we were together?"

"No," Glen said fiercely. "He said you start out light and get rough, and I let my imagination get the better of me. I'm looking for a way out of this because it's too goddamned perfect and no one gets second chances like this."

He tried to push away but Derek wouldn't let him. "Beautiful baby boy…sometimes deserving people do get a second chance. And a third. A fourth."

Glen's nostrils flared a little but he didn't say anything more.

"I'll let you go if that's what you need. What you want. But just know it's not what I want."

"It's not what I want either. I'm sorry—I haven't had anyone for so long and I didn't mean to undermine you with Mark or coming in here alone."

"You didn't do anything of the sort." Derek held him tight. "I meant every word I said."

Glen bowed his head against him, waiting. "Did he hurt you?"

Derek wasn't giving Glen the option of not answering.

"Back then, he did. Physically. Emotionally. Partially my fault. I just wasn't up for it."

"Not your fault. He should've known."

Glen squared his shoulders in a military set and he nodded. "You would've." "I already do know."

"I'm afraid I won't be enough for you."

In another life, the level of non-submission wouldn't have been. But Derek was older, wiser, realized that the submission Glen gave was better and hotter than anything he'd ever experienced. The boy challenged him, made him realize what he'd been missing. "You're fucking perfect for me, Glen. If you'll have me." "Jesus, yes." Glen nuzzled his neck. "Take me home, tie me up and take me any way you want. Please."

"It's the 'please' that's going to get your bossy ass off the hook every time." Glen smiled like he knew.

Derek took him out of the club fast after that—although the ride seemed to take forever, Glen managed to appear patient.

Derek put a hand on his crotch. Hadn't let Glen wipe the come off himself and he squirmed with anticipation as Derek chuckled softly.

Whatever the man had planned for him, Glen couldn't wait any longer. The first orgasm hasn't even taken the edge off. Now, his need clawed at him, like he knew Derek could give him what no one else had. And before Derek let him inside, he was half wrapped around Derek, letting the man ravage his mouth, tonguing him until he couldn't take it any longer. His shirt was off as he slammed the door shut behind him—and after Derek walked him to the bedroom, he stripped his jeans as Derek undressed as well.

"Lie back," he told Glen, who moved toward the headboard. Out of his jacket pocket, he took condoms, lube and leather cuffs.

Jesus, his cock got hard at the sight. Derek knew, gave him a small smile, like he was happy he pleased Glen. And that gave Glen both a heady sense of pleasure and power he'd never felt before. He'd never even thought about what really got a Dom off, until right now.

He was doing it, and that made everything he did tonight brand new, like he was some kind of blushing virgin. Except this time, he knew exactly what he was doing.

"Hands on the headboard," Derek instructed, and Glen complied with the authority in the man's voice, his cock jutting at the command. The cuffs strapped to his wrists made him harder and the ones on his ankles, spreading his legs and holding him fast to the bed, made him want to come immediately. Derek bent to lick the come off his stomach, and it was so goddamned dirty and hot. He heard a keening groan escape his throat when Derek deep-throated his cock.

He hadn't been told to come. His arms and legs were immobile, his hips held down by Derek's body, his cock a prisoner to Derek's hot mouth, and the stress of the night—of the mission—all began to fall away like heavy blocks from his body.

He was floating—unable to move his hips, he contented himself with the sensations. And Derek tongued his slit until he couldn't stand it any longer. He looked down and saw Derek staring up at him, saw Derek's nod and came in hot spurts into Derek's mouth.

Before he could even recover, Derek's body covered his, and the man bent his head to kiss Glen so he tasted himself and the whiskey Derek had drunk earlier.

"You taste so. Fucking. Good," he groaned against Glen's mouth. "Like candy."

"Let me taste you," Glen asked.

Derek complied, straddling Glen's face, but told him, "I'm coming inside your ass, not your mouth."

He couldn't stop watching Glen's face, Glen's mouth stretched around his cock, taking what he wanted, but those eyes…as he stared up at Derek, he only wanted to please.

Derek would let him. Ran his hands through the man's hair and then tugged it roughly, feeling Glen's moan of approval hum around his cock. "Beautiful baby," he murmured.

There was the hum again and then a scrape of teeth against his head, which made Derek groan and buck, and yes, the boy would pay for that, in a way that was enjoyable for both.

He pulled out of Glen's mouth and mounted him. "Going to fuck you senseless," he promised.

Glen nodded. Blew out a hard breath as Derek breached the first ring of muscle. Derek didn't pause, entered the younger man slowly until he was balls- deep. And only then did he let Glen adjust to the girth. Nipped his shoulders until he saw the tension drop and felt Glen push back a little against him.

"Yeah," Glen breathed. "Fuck me, Derek. Please…I need…"

They both did. Derek rocked into him, both men groaning in their collective pleasure. Derek hadn't realized how badly he needed, too. Was so pissed that he hadn't told Glen not to come looking for him in the club alone before that. Hated seeing the anger and fear in the boy's eyes.

"Lick my pit while I'm buried deep in your ass," Derek told him. Glen's face went into his armpit and he began to lick without hesitation. Derek continued to pound him, holding him in a completely submissive position where the boy could barely move.

He heard Glen's moans of pleasure, and his own balls tightened—if he hadn't tied Glen down, they would no doubt be on the floor right now, and as it was, the bed was making a dangerous sound, like it wouldn't survive this night.

Derek plowed into Glen several more times, hitting Glen's prostate at just the right angle to make the boy shoot uncontrollably.

Glen passed out after he came. It wasn't for a long time, but when he opened his eyes, Derek was lying next to him and his wrists were untied—and unmarked. But Derek was massaging them lightly anyway.

"You all right?" he asked.

Glen nodded. "I didn't mean to doubt you earlier."

He put a finger under Glen's chin. "You doubted yourself."

It was the truth. Derek delivered it without being a know-it-all, did it so matter-of-factly that Glen didn't feel silly or stupid at all.

He was getting exactly what he needed. And, in a short period of time, he was the happiest he'd been in he didn't know how long. "Thank you."

"For what?"

"For making me feel like a man."

Derek just got it—got him so completely. "You should always feel that   way.

Just because you need someone doesn't make you weak."

That was a concept Glen still couldn't wrap his mind around.

"It's hard to let go of what you thought you needed," he admitted. "For a long time, I hung on to swimming because that's what I was good at. Because I was told I had a gift that would be a shame to waste. It made my parents happy. Kept them proud of me, even after I told them I was gay. But when I met John, everything clicked. I'm just sorry I used that as an excuse to quit. If I hadn't been such a coward, I would've done that years earlier."

"I doubt John thought you were a coward. I certainly don't. Christ, Glen, you were a kid. Sometimes it takes people a hell of a lot longer to come to those realizations."

At Derek's words, Glen felt the pressure inside him ease. He could trust Derek to be honest with him. He'd pretty much known that from day one.

Maybe lightning could strike twice. After all, Derek was still missing his sub as well. What if…

"You're thinking so hard I can smell the wood burning," Derek teased, and Glen swore as a blush rose hot on his cheeks, a trait that Derek seemed to enjoy way too much.

"Then you'd better do something about it," Glen told him, which earned him a swat on the ass before he was dragged into the steam shower.

After Derek got Glen dirtier in the shower—and then cleaned them both up after fucking him against the tile wall, he realized Glen's stomach was growling like no one's business.

He threw the man a towel as he hurriedly dried himself. "I've got steaks— grab whatever you need and meet me downstairs."

He pulled on jeans and a flannel shirt that he didn't bother to button, went to the kitchen and pulled out the meat and some potatoes to grill. Found fresh green beans he'd gotten as well.

Glen joined him in a pair of borrowed sweats, bare feet

and chest.

"I'll throw them on the grill," he told Derek, took the platter, shoved his feet into his boots and went out to start the grill in the cold. Derek watched him from the window, admiring the way the boy's muscles flexed. Derek was no slouch, but Glen trained daily. He'd noted bruises on the boy that he hoped were from training and not real-life experience, although Derek knew better than to ask. Navy pilots were trained like they'd be dropped and left in enemy territory. Derek remembered similar training in the Marines.

The decision to leave the military wasn't an easy one. But fifteen years had been enough. These days, he taught self-defense and weaponry to corporate types and would- be bodyguards who traveled to dangerous places.

Since he'd lost Jared, he'd been lonely as hell. He'd gone to the bar four months after because he'd needed a release. Found some nice guys but no one who did it for him the way Glen did.

He thought about Glen's earlier words—*It's hard to let go of what you thought you needed…*

So goddamned true. And the boy had definitely been patient enough. So after they'd eaten and were relaxing on the couch, he started, "Jared was the name of my sub who died. We were together for four years until he died. A car accident. We'd had a fight and he stormed out."

He put his head down, because even now he could slip into blaming himself so easily. "We didn't live together—that was always a sticking point between us.

But deep down, even though we loved each other, I don't think either of us wanted to take that step. I was still in the military—I didn't want to deal with the scrutiny."

But really, that was an excuse.

"At least you were honest about it with him," Glen said.

"Even so, I stayed in something so I didn't have to push myself or go outside my comfort zone," he admitted.

"And now?"

"I want more. I think I've found it." He brushed a hand over Glen's cheek. "The sub Mark was talking about... I took him on after Jared. He was really into pain. I didn't scar him, but I gave him what he wanted, even though it wasn't my thing. So Mark was right—I hurt my sub, but he forgot to mention that it's exactly what my sub wanted."

"I guess we both did stupid things out of grief."

"Yeah. But I think what we're doing now is a good thing."

"Even though... Are you getting what you want by doing what I want?" Glen asked. "Because if you're not—"

"It's exactly what I want," Derek told him, and for the first time in a long time, he truly meant it.

6

The following weekend, Glen met him at his house instead of the bar. Derek thought it best for them to get some more time alone under their belt before going back there. He wanted the boy to be on firm footing.

Truth be told, he wanted Glen all to himself, wanted to be selfish with their time together, since he didn't know when or for how long another mission would take the boy away from him.

He left the door open, sat on the couch with a beer and the book he'd been reading. Glen knocked lightly and came in, sat next to him on the couch after taking off his sneakers.

He put his head back on the seat and closed his eyes as he settled in comfortably. He wore loose, ripped-up jeans and a T-shirt, and there were more bruises on him.

Derek went into the kitchen and brought him back a Coke, because he wanted the boy awake. "Rough one?"

Glen nodded, his eyes still closed. "But sometimes it just helps you to know you're alive."

Derek put a hand on Glen's thigh and Glen grinned. The

boy was much lighter than he'd been, and if Derek were honest with himself, so was he. Glen had to have noticed it too.

"What about you? Long day?" Glen asked after he downed half the soda. "Christmas shopping," Derek admitted and Glen rolled his eyes. "What?

You're not into Christmas?"

"Haven't celebrated it in years. Why start again now?" "Because you didn't have me then."

Glen opened his eyes and Derek watched him bite back a smart-ass answer.

Instead, he just touched Derek's cheek but didn't say anything.

He hadn't bought Glen anything, but he definitely had a gift in mind for him—in fact, the boy had been in his thoughts most of the week. But he didn't push the Christmas talk now, instead told Glen, "You want to be tied tighter. Held more strongly. You crave that."

"Yes."

With that confirmation, he planned on giving Glen exactly what he wanted— what he wanted too. The feel of that strong, muscled body below him, all that power, gentled just for him and him alone. Gave himself over to Derek for safekeeping, and that was a task Derek didn't take lightly.

"I want to do something to you," he told the boy. "Like what?"

Derek smiled, wickedly enough to make Glen's stomach feel like it was full of nerves. He finished the soda, then stood and stripped. "Okay, then do it."

Derek didn't hem and haw, ordered him upstairs. Brought him to the second bedroom, where leather cuffs hung down from a hook on the ceiling. "Arms up." Glen swallowed, complied and Derek tied his wrists tight. Kicked his legs open and reached for the spreader bar on the table. Clamped each ankle so he

couldn't move anything, could barely sway his body.

Derek started with his nipples—a squeeze and then a lick, until Glen was squirming.

It was only then when Derek snapped the leather cock ring into place.

"No," Glen heard himself moan but Derek's tongue was already flicking his nipples again. "You said no punishments."

"Why do you look on pleasure as a punishment?" Derek asked, and Glen couldn't answer that at all.

The clamps went on each nipple—Glen's body broke out in a fine sheen of sweat.

"You like that, baby?" "Yes."

"That's yes, Sir."

"Yes, Sir." Glen's whole body vibrated from the complete lack of control. It was all sensation—he could feel his skin prickle from the air, and he wanted to float away with Derek right now.

Glen wanted to beg, but he forced himself not to. His body was strung tight and not just because of the expert bindings. Derek's face was flushed with sex...lust... And the feeling of being wanted—really wanted—was like a drug Glen wanted more of.

Derek's hand ran along the crack of his ass. He entered Glen with a lubed finger to loosen him—and then progressed quickly to two and then three—stood behind him, nipping his shoulder. Murmured, "Could leave you here like this. Or maybe we could do this at the club—put you on display."

He wasn't able to do much more than buck his ass into Derek's hand, but Derek put a stop to that with an arm wrapped around his chest. He couldn't move, could barely breathe, and the pleasure built to a nearly unbearable level.

And when Derek continued talking, he knew he was close to losing it.

"After we're done, I think I'm going to shave you...and then everyone will know you're mine. And they definitely will when I lock you in a cock cage."

The groan was a keening wail that continued as Derek drove his cock inside him, unlocking the cock ring as he did so. And Glen let himself be taken. Claimed. Filled to his limits. And then taken past them, further than he'd thought possible.

Ridden. Fucked, and allowed to love it.

"More," was all he could say, and Derek gave him

everything he could handle. His body was a slave to Derek's hands, his mouth, his whims for the night. A blur of incredible sensation.

And again, the feeling of wanting to hold Derek while he came hit him. Just picturing himself doing that threw him over the edge. The intensity of the orgasm increased as Derek released the nipple clamps, barely aware of how loudly he was yelling—and not at all sure what he was actually saying.

It didn't matter. All that did was Derek.

At some point, Derek released his arms and carried him to the bed, removed the spreader bar but chained him facedown so he could fuck him again. Glen just swam in a sea of warm contentment.

Glen turned his head for a moment to look at him, a contented glow on his cheeks.

"Dirty little boy," he murmured, and Glen nodded, a gleam in his eye, and Derek felt the emotion hit him like a sharp punch he'd been on the receiving end of in boot camp. This time, the pain was far more worth it.

He'd fallen in goddamned love fast and hard, and had probably started the second he'd seen Glen come into the bar. Wanted him with his heart and soul.

For Glen, Derek realized, it wasn't about the pain. In his job, he liked to fly out of control but during sex, he liked to be in one place, held still and comforted.

He was in love with the man. And right now, he didn't give a shit about anything else. Not with Glen tied and spread facedown on the bed, ass open and ready for anything Derek wanted to do to him.

And what Derek wanted was the boy's arms wrapped around him, but he took him this way instead, loving the way Glen responded to the fucking. He pumped into Glen and they came within seconds of each other.

They cleaned up, showered off with Derek basically holding Glen up under the spray. The boy was relaxed and happy, and sleepy. When he brought him back to bed, he pulled off the blanket they'd dirtied and slipped into clean sheets. Glen was back against the pillows, his eyes heavy, a small smile of contentment on his mouth. Derek kissed him, drawing him in so the boy could taste himself. "Sleep now, beautiful boy."

"I'm off tomorrow."

"I don't have work either," he told Glen.

"Good—that leaves you time for more shopping," Glen teased.

"I'm all done, wiseass." He rolled on his back and watched the snow fall outside his bedroom window. Glen's legs were still trembling and Derek turned back to rub them as Glen moaned quietly. Contentedly.

"You all right or do you need more?"

Glen snorted. "Think I'm all right. For now."

Derek pulled him closer, stroked a hand down his back. "Listen, if you're not working…you can come home with me for Christmas."

Glen stared up at him like he had a million heads. Derek cleared his throat and started again, feeling like a nervous kid inviting a new friend to a birthday party. "I'd like my mom to meet you—it'll just be for a few days."

"I, ah…" Glen shifted. "I probably have to work."

He was lying, but Derek let it go. "Okay. Well, if things change, feel free to come home with me, all right?"

Glen pulled away from him, sat on the edge of the bed and didn't look at Derek when he said, "They won't. Besides, I don't celebrate it anymore—I told you that."

"So you didn't spend Christmas with John?" he couldn't help but ask. At his words, Glen was up, looking for his clothes on the floor, pulling them on, and Derek didn't try to stop him. Knew he couldn't.

"Sometimes I was there on Christmas, but we didn't sit down and open presents or anything. He never pressured me about it." Glen's last words stung a little, something of an accusation.

"Sometimes I'm afraid I can't live up to him."

"I'm not asking you to be John. I'm not looking for a replacement. If I'd come back into the bar earlier than this, I would've been. Now, I'm looking for a Dom who gets me. Who doesn't expect to be served. Who wants me for me, not just because I was John's sub." Glen paused. "By the way, just so you know, you lived up to him just fine."

    With that, the boy left, the door swinging behind him.

7

Glen had been away a week on this last mission, had gotten called in the night he'd stormed out of Derek's house, which he thought was pretty damned serendipitous.

Now, it was nearly Christmas and he was home earlier than he'd thought.

When he was finally debriefed, he dragged his ass home.

It had been a rough one. Everyone was hurt in some form or another. He'd helped save one of the guys, flown through some serious fire.

It didn't hit him until he was alone. It started with the chills and he wondered if it was a side effect of the shit they injected him with when he returned. The next thing he knew, it was ten hours later and he'd passed out on the couch, woke up sweating.

He called the doc, who confirmed Glen wasn't the only one who'd gotten sick. That didn't make him feel particularly better, but he was at least glad he'd stocked his kitchen with basics that wouldn't spoil before he left at the beginning of the month. Not that he felt like eating, but he knew he needed something in his stomach.

Which he promptly threw up. Fuck.

Derek was going home for Christmas. For all he knew, he was already there.

Or preparing. Or shopping or some shit.

He didn't know why all of that made him so pissed, but it did. Which was why he didn't call the man. At least not right away.

You should call him.

But what would that mean? Sure, Derek was always there for him where sex was concerned, but this was a whole other level. Glen didn't like admitting vulnerability outside of sex because doing it while being tied down was enough.

In the end, he wrestled with it for another half a day before texting him. Left the ball in Derek's court.

Derek called him immediately. "Did you just get in?" "Yeah."

"What the hell's wrong with you?" he demanded and Glen paused before admitting, "Think I'm sick."

"I'll be right over."

"You don't have to do that."

"Don't you tell me what I have to do," Derek said. "How long have you been sick and alone?"

"I thought…" Damn, he was close to a panic attack. He'd fucked up and all he could do was close his eyes, the phone still pressed to his ear. "I thought…"

"You weren't thinking. I'll be right over."

When he got Glen's text, Derek's evening had definitely looked up. After he'd spoken to the boy, he was angry as hell but had packed a bag and gotten into his car immediately. For Glen—for any guy—to admit he was sick meant he was pretty close to death's door.

But the fact that he'd waited so long to call… Well, the trust between them definitely needed further work.

He knocked for ten minutes, getting progressively more worried, until he heard the lock move and Glen, wrapped in a blanket, opened the door.

"Jesus." He took the boy in hand, dropped his bag, closed the door somehow all at once. "How long have you been like this?"

"Couple of days," Glen admitted.

"When you're better, I'll spank the shit out of you for not calling me sooner," Derek murmured, his tone gentle but his words serious.

"Not that bad."

"Bullshit." He didn't need to take a temp to know Glen's was high—the boy was radiating enough heat to keep Chernobyl running. He guided him to the bedroom, sat him on the edge of the bed and ran a bath for him, keeping the temperature neutral. Got him stripped down—and shivering—and put him in.

Glen resisted a little—"Not a pussy," he muttered—but Derek was insistent, and finally the boy settled into the tub, where Derek sponged his skin from burning hot to a more satisfactory cooler temp. Glen remained still under his touch, his head back against the towel Derek folded for his comfort, eyes closed. He didn't think the mood had anything to do with Glen's flu. But as the boy got more comfortable, he settled in and finally opened his eyes with a drowsy look on his face,

"Didn't mean to make you mad," he said.

"Too late." But the anger had long dissipated. Glen was too sick—too stressed—and Derek would never forgive himself if something happened to this boy.

His boy. Because he wasn't looking for just any sub, but rather, someone who would sub for him and him alone. Who would surrender to him in ways Glen wouldn't for anyone else. "I'm not just here for you for sex, all right? I thought you got that."

Glen shrugged, like he didn't want to deal with it.

"Stay put—I'm changing your sheets." He walked away before Glen could argue, stripped the bed and made it quickly. Dumped the dirty laundry in the washing machine, collected ginger ale and crackers from the kitchen and went to fetch the boy.

There was already Tylenol on the night table. He didn't know if Glen needed a doctor or if he'd seen one on base, but those would be his next questions.

He grabbed a pair of sweats and brought them into the bathroom. "Let's get you cleaned up and into bed."

"Thanks," Glen murmured, shifted so the water splashed around him a little. "You haven't seen anything yet." Derek soaped him up, washed his hair and rinsed him off with the reverence he'd only held for one other person. And when Glen stood on shaky legs, the fever still obvious in his flushed cheeks, he walked with him to the bedroom. He took Glen's temperature—still 101 despite the cooling.

The boy was just about the get into bed when his cell rang. He sat on the edge of the bed and took the call, which ended up being from the doctor on base. Reported his fever and then said, "No, I'm not alone. I have a friend of mine. He's taking care...yeah."

He held out the phone and Derek took it to listen to the doc's instructions, which included a brusque recap of *it's the flu, no antibiotics, keep his damned fever down and don't let him do anything stupid.* "Got it."

"No improvement—or if he gets worse—call. You'll have to bring him in," Doc said. "I expect this will last another twenty-four hours, at least."

Don't ask, don't tell, but they had no reason to assume he was anything but a friend...and he was.

He handed the phone back to Glen, who assured the doctor that he wouldn't overdo it, and then the boy hung up and crawled into bed.

"Are you staying?" he asked Derek. "Whether you want

me to or not."

"Sorry...didn't mean to worry you. Hate being sick." He buried his face in Derek's shoulder as chills racked his body again.

"It happens to the best of us."

"Not to me. I wasn't allowed to be sick," he admitted. "Couldn't be sick or scared or tired. Couldn't lose. Needed the winner's mindset all the damned time."

He didn't sound bitter, just very matter-of-fact, which, to Derek, made it worse. "Sounds intense."

"It was all I knew." Glen shifted, kicked the covers off restlessly. "Fever's breaking."

Derek went and grabbed another cool washcloth from the bathroom and rubbed Glen's face and chest as he lay back against the pillows.

"When I met John, I was at the breaking point. The swimming wasn't doing it for me. I was losing focus. Something else was driving me."

"And John brought it out for you."

"Yeah." Glen's voice sounded far away, halfway between sleep and memory.

Derek let him drift off, suddenly too caught up in his own memories...and worries.

He was a good Dom. A good man. But living up to John...

Glen didn't even call you when he was sick.

That had hit him like a physical blow.

Derek handed him the glass of soda. "Drink. Take your

pills. And just relax." "An order?"

"Direct."

Glen barely got the pills down before he was asleep. Derek's flight home was booked for the next morning—two days before Christmas Eve. He moved it twenty-four hours ahead, would play it by ear, because there was no way he was leaving Glen this sick and alone.

Now wasn't the time to bug Glen about coming home with him, either. Derek had accepted that wouldn't happen, pretty much assumed Glen would still be away over the holidays, too. No doubt, Glen would be the one to volunteer to work so pilots with families could be with them.

He brushed some damp hair from Glen's forehead as he sat next to him on the bed. Switched on the TV and tried to figure out who he was angrier at— himself or the boy.

In the end, he decided it was his fault and ended up taking Glen's hand in his.

He was dreaming—and he was stripping from the incredible heat. Maybe his helo crashed and he was crawling in the desert looking for help. He called out but didn't recognize his own voice.

"Glen, come on, it's all right."

Derek.

Derek was touching his head, whispering. Fuck. Glen was

hot and cold…remembered that he was down with the flu, that he was home in his own bed.

"Glen, you with me?"

He opened his eyes and stared up at Derek. He couldn't say anything, but it didn't matter. Derek was in control, taking care of him. Cooling him, heating him…not leaving his side. He knew he slept, but for how long, he wasn't sure.

But finally, he was awake and, although still dizzy, he was able to open his eyes for longer than a minute or two.

"Hey, bud." Derek ran a hand through his own hair. He looked tired. "How long have you been here?"

"A little over twenty-four hours. You said you'd been back for a couple of days, though."

"Yeah." He accepted a long drink of fizzy soda before lying back on the pillows. Remembered talking, and then he was back asleep.

And then he realized he could hear the strains of an argument. He didn't know if it was day or night—or what day it actually was—because the fever still held him in its grip.

But when he heard the words, "What are you doing with my son?" it was as if he was seventeen years old again and getting caught in John's apartment.

He'd been half-dressed, his ass sore from the much-needed spanking John had recently delivered, coming out of the bedroom.

John answered the door in only a towel, and yeah, it looked bad. Looked exactly like what you'd think happened just happened, and Glen was frozen to the spot, staring at his mother standing there.

"Glen Michael Rhodes, what are you doing?" The look on her face was anger blended with disgust.

And still, he couldn't speak. John had asked her to leave immediately but she refused.

"He's coming home with me," his mother said.

"No." John held firm, even when she'd threatened him with the police. Maybe he, like Glen, knew she'd never embarrass herself with a court case of that nature.

That evening, for the first time in nine years, Glen didn't go to swim practice, spent the night curled in John's bed, scared to go home and not sure how to go forward.

Eventually, he got up and pushed the covers aside. Went home and had the huge, blow-out fight with his parents he'd expected, packed and went back to John's.

He'd enlisted in the Navy three months later on his eighteenth birthday. He'd tried to keep swimming—John encouraged it, said he'd help finance it as well—but Glen's heart was no longer in it. Truth be told, he wasn't sure it ever had been.

Now, he forced himself out of bed. It was dark out and he stumbled a little as he headed toward the voices.

His worst nightmare had indeed forced her way into his townhouse and Derek was telling her to keep her voice down.

"And who are you?"

"I'm his friend," Derek told her diplomatically while Glen

waited in the shadows of the hallway, wishing the whole damned thing would go away.

"Friend?" she sneered. "I know what *friend* means to your kind of people." "I'll bet you do," Derek continued in his unflinchingly calm tone that must be making his mother angrier.

He couldn't let this happen again. And this time, Glen found his footing, moved forward with a purpose he finally understood and told her, "Get the hell out of here."

She turned and stared at him. "You can't talk to me like that."

"I just did. I cut you off the way you cut me off," he told her. "We have no more relationship."

"I'm trying to save you, Glen Michael. I don't want you to burn in hell for this...lifestyle. A good man would repent," she pleaded. The sickening part of all of it was that she truly believed this bullshit.

Derek's stance didn't change—but he looked right at Glen even though his words were directed to Glen's mother. "Your son is probably the best man I know. I'm honored to be a part of his life. And you can leave now."

"You'll burn in hell too."

"I guess we'll be seeing you there," Derek said.

She turned her fury from Glen to Derek. "You men corrupted my son. He wasn't born like this."

He had been—and there was nothing more to say, except, "If you leave now, I won't call the police."

Derek pointed, went to put a light hand on her shoulder to guide her out of the front hallway and she flinched. "Don't you touch me."

"It's not contagious, you know," Glen said. "Or maybe it is." With that, she turned her icy facade to the outside and left.

"I'm guessing I just met one of your good reasons for not wanting anything to do with parents," Derek said.

All Glen could do was nod. He wanted to apologize, but it was as if all the strength had been zapped from his body.

He thought they could never humiliate him again, but he'd obviously been wrong, and still, Derek had handled it so well.

"You didn't deserve that," he said tiredly. "Neither did you," Derek said.

Glen nodded, because he wasn't sure of much, but that he did know. "Sorry."

"S'okay."

"They're religious. Middle-class. My father had no tolerance for anyone who wasn't like them. So they never practiced what they preached." Swimming would've been a way out of the small town for him—which was exactly the escape he'd wanted. Or so he thought.

Instead, he'd moved two towns over after he'd saved enough money to move off base. Didn't feel guilty about not getting out, because in so many important ways, he had.

8

Derek took a few deep breaths because he didn't want Glen to see how close to over-the-edge angry he was that a mother could treat her son that way. Didn't want Glen to think for one second that he was angry at him for anything his mother did or said. He wished he could've saved Glen from hearing any of that.

Glen, who stood in the doorway, bare-chested. His cheeks were flushed from fever—anger—his body language reading tight and defensive. "Why now after all this time?" he muttered.

"Promise of the end of the world brings out the insanity in some people." "She never needed an excuse."

The anger would come out now, mainly to cover the shame. But Derek had to tread carefully. The fever still had Glen in its grips—he wouldn't be thinking all that rationally anyway but coupled with something this extreme happening… "Why don't you get back into bed—get some more sleep?"

"Can't sleep now." Glen shrugged. There was a sudden look of defiance in his eyes that made Derek want to hug him…and put him over his knee.

"You can't let her get to you."

"She's been doing it for years. Just when I think I've made it out, she shows up to berate me about who I am or what I am. So don't tell me to not let her get to me like it's so goddamned easy. It's great that your family's so accepting, but you haven't lived through what I have, so don't pretend you know everything."

"Don't do this, Glen."

"What?" He brushed past Derek and headed to the couch. It didn't take a genius to figure out that, for the boy, seeing her made all the old feelings rush back. It wasn't the gay part Glen was ashamed of—it was no doubt the kink. Why he'd never been able to let it go…why he needed it so badly…and that was something Derek wanted to help him deal with.

"It's not her—it's you. You're the problem."

"Then get the fuck out," Glen told him. "Because I sure as hell don't want to be your problem."

"You're pushing your luck with me, boy."

Glen's chin jutted. "Like I said, then leave. I'm not asking you to handle this."

"But I'm doing it anyway. It doesn't matter if she never accepts you. You have to accept yourself," Derek said.

"Put it on a greeting card," Glen muttered, and that was exactly what Derek wanted to hear.

"I gave you the rope and you just hung yourself," he growled and then he moved to action.

Glen immediately regretted his words, saw the look in Derek's eyes and knew he was in for it. Before he could back away, Derek had him in a hold, had him cuffed and helpless before he could utter any kind of apology. But the hold made him angrier and he fought, told Derek to get the fuck off him.

"Not a chance, little boy," Derek told him. And then the man had him over his knee—he had the element of surprise on his side, plus he made use of the fact that Glen wasn't exactly steady on his feet yet.

"No—not like this." Glen struggled, but his sweats pulled down easily and Derek's hand met his ass with a hard slap.

"I'm not doing this to punish you for what happened. I'm doing this to stop you from doubting yourself, your choices. None of this is wrong. I'm not letting you up until you realize it."

Glen howled, part anger, part regret, and he fought too. Might've won with a lesser Dom or if his wrists weren't tied, but luck wasn't on his side.

Derek's bare hand met bare bottom again and again with a thwack that reverberated through his soul, and no, it wasn't the way it had been with John, but it wasn't the way it had been with Mark either. It was better than it had ever been. Derek was good at this. Better than good, he realized when the measured slaps had him sinking into that place where pleasure mingled with pain, melding into one until he couldn't see straight.

Until he didn't care about anything else but the pleasure.

He wasn't sure when it stopped or when the orgasm shot through him, because that hadn't been his goal. All the pain, anger, grief poured out of him until there was nothing left but pure, unadulterated pleasure.

And while he was still in the throes of his orgasm, Derek was picking him up, putting him over the back of the couch, bent him forward so he couldn't move. And still, Derek kept a hand on the back of his neck, tight.

Derek thrust hard, over and over without stopping, giving Glen no time to recover from the constant intense pleasure of his cock jutting against Glen's prostate.

This sex was dirty. Hot. Hard and fast and slow and depraved. Glen begged for everything he got wantonly. Watched Derek love giving it to him, heard Derek say, "There's nothing wrong with wanting it like this. Never was."

Glen was aware that he was yelling—probably nonsense in between groans, and then it was like he blacked out as his cock pumped out come like he'd been celibate for years.

He was aware of Derek helping him up. Murmuring, his breath soothing against Glen's too-warm skin. Everything ached, including his head, but Derek wasn't going to push away that easily. Held him, stroked him, until he remembered how good what was supposed to be so bad felt.

When he was finally completely pliant in his arms, Derek took him into the bedroom.

"That's it…come on, give yourself over to me again," Derek

encouraged as he positioned them in front of the mirror on the outside of the closed closet door, with Glen standing in front of him. Glen let his head fall back, watched them in the mirror as Derek's hand slid up and down his cock, taking him the way Glen wanted.

Derek's cock rubbed against him, but he didn't fuck him again, simply jerked Glen off as Glen gasped and jolted.

"Hold yourself still," Derek demanded. Glen did, but it wasn't enough. Not until Derek pushed him to the wall, and Glen held his palms out on opposite sides of the mirror to brace himself. Let Derek pull another orgasm from him, this one making him relax totally. And then Derek had him again, held him up, wrapped him tight. Cleaned them both in the shower as the dazed sleep settled in.

When he woke sometime the next afternoon, he was curled around Derek as if he were protecting the Dom.

Derek didn't seem to mind, was sleeping peacefully. Glen moved down and took his cock in his mouth—he hardened immediately.

"Beautiful baby," he murmured as Glen began to worship his body, kissed his way down, nipping and sucking and marking his Dom, making Derek groan when his tongue licked the head of his cock. Glen deep-throated him as Derek's fingers threaded through his hair.

"Come fuck your daddy," he said, pointed to his lap. Glen stripped…lowered himself, poised to slide himself down on Derek's cock. When Derek touched his ass cheeks with his hands, Glen winced, which was good. He'd remember.

"Gently, baby—you'll be sore," Derek reminded him, because the sex between them had been hard and fast. But this one would be different. Glen would take the lead and it was soft and slow. He lowered himself gingerly onto Derek's cock, both of them moaning as he finally took Derek completely inside of him.

And, for the first time since they'd been together, Glen didn't worry about being bound. Wrapped his arms around Derek's broad shoulders, held the man the way he'd wanted to while they made love—quiet and intense—even as the storm began to howl around them. It shook the house the way Derek had shaken Glen up.

And it was fucking perfect.

In the aftermath, Derek lay on his back with Glen curled around him again. He stroked his hand along the boy's naked back. So much baggage put to rest behind them. Today felt like a new start for both of them.

Glen spoke first. "Until last night…I didn't realize…tying me really gets you off."

"You couldn't tell that before this?"

"I wanted to make sure. I mean, you don't want to be tied or anything?"

"I'm content tying you," he told Glen. "What you're

doing—what we're doing—is enough for me. More than. I told you—I'll tie you whenever and however you need it."

"It's one of the only times all the noise in my head stops—the worry, the fear, the stress, the day-to-day shit. Holding me so I can't move quiets me. Weird, right?"

"No, it's not. Makes sense." Derek hugged him. "And I love giving it to you."

"Even though I'm a complete pain in the ass, right?"

"Fights are a normal part of a relationship." Derek paused. "I'd like to think that's what we have."

Glen nodded. "I guess I suck at it." "Sucking is one of your finer qualities."

"Asshole," Glen muttered. "You really think you can handle me? Deal with all my shit?"

"I don't think your baggage is the problem. Just fucking accept that your kink is being tied. From there, the rest should be easy."

After all the man had done for him, Derek asked so little in return. And Glen still couldn't bring himself to go to the man's family for Christmas.

He felt like he was saying no to the relationship, but he didn't want to lie anymore. "I knew I'd be home for Christmas."

"I guess you had a really good reason to lie about it," Derek said.

Dammit, this was hard. It would be so much easier to walk away. "I wasn't ready to talk about my reasons."

"But then it walked through the door." Derek's gaze was

steady. "Can you blame me?"

"Never. I know I can tell you my family's not like that and you're not ready to believe it. I can accept that, but fuck, no one should be alone on Christmas."

"I'll be okay. You won't be gone long. And I want this to work. Don't want to let you go."

"Then don't."

Glen responded to Derek by kissing him, holding on to the back of his neck like he didn't want to give the man the chance—or the option—of getting away. Derek let that slide because he really enjoyed the possessiveness in the boy. Shit like that really turned him on…and he had a feeling Glen had that figured out as well.

9

The next morning, Glen felt like his old self. Better than, maybe. His ass was sore and he rubbed it as he got out of bed.

He heard Derek on the phone with the airlines.

"I'll take anything. Doesn't matter if it's connecting." He paused. "Yeah, no, it's Christmas Eve. I get it."

He hung up, ran his hands through his hair, elbows on the table. His back was so tense, Glen stepped forward and began to massage his shoulders. Derek let out an appreciative groan as Glen's fingers dug in. "No flight?"

"Nothing."

"You didn't book ahead of time?"

"I did," he said quietly and Glen realized that Derek had given up his airline seat to stay with him and nurse him back to health.

"I'm going to drive. If I leave now, I'll make it by morning," he said, like it was completely reasonable. And maybe it would've been, if a storm hadn't been ravaging the Eastern Seaboard and promised to continue doing so for at least twenty-four more hours.

"Where is home?" "Vermont." "Jesus, Derek…"

"I'll be fine," he said. "But the offer to come home with me still stands. It's beautiful there. Quiet. Simple."

"But your parents—"

"My mom and sister. They already know about you." "What do they know?"

"That I'm more than halfway to loving you."

Derek said it so easily, but there was a guardedness in his eyes that Glen recognized. The man didn't trust him, not fully, not to break his heart.

It was the last thing Glen wanted to do. "I'm sorry—it's just not my thing." "So you'd rather be alone on Christmas?"

"It's been that way for long enough that I stopped noticing." "Maybe I want you to notice."

Glen paused and then asked, "What did your mother and sister say, when you told them that about me?"

"That they hadn't heard me sound that happy in a long time."

He didn't look happy now. Glen hated to think he was responsible for that. Not when this man had brought him back from the dead in the space of mere months when no one had been able to do it in years. Or maybe ever. "Not going to be an easy drive."

"I'll be fine. I like being at home. My mom's been fighting breast cancer for years. I don't get to see her enough as it is. She doesn't complain, but having me home for Christmas…" He trailed off. "It's all right, Glen. I'm not upset. We'll talk as soon as I get back, all right?"

"Call when you get there."

"I can do that." He packed up his stuff and gave Glen a fierce kiss. "I get it— you've had too much parenting for a lifetime. Don't worry—I'll be fine."

Glen watched as Derek cleared snow off his truck—he'd refused to let Glen out to help him. "Not letting you get sick when you've just recovered," he'd said. And finally, the truck was free and clear and Derek backed out of the driveway. Glen remained staring at the empty space where it had remained for days.

Was he really ready to let things end like this? Derek said he'd call when he returned—Glen didn't doubt that, didn't think this was some kind of test…but if he couldn't do this small thing for Derek, what else couldn't he do?

Maybe he wouldn't return the call after Christmas. Give Derek the easy way out.

Easy way out for you too. And you'll be alone again.

That wouldn't be so bad if he didn't know that Derek was so right for him.

More than anyone, more than John, even, and the fact that he could admit it— mean it—hit him hard enough to make him sink to the floor for a few minutes. He had to force himself to breathe at the enormity of what he'd just realized.

He wrapped his arms around his knees as he curled into a ball. Smelled Derek all over him.

All Derek wanted was, well, something most people could

do without a problem. A family visit. But family…

He could fly death-defying things, but the thought of moving forward paralyzed him. And how the hell long could he allow fear to fuck with him?

He closed his eyes and pictured Derek—the night they'd met. The night the Dom had intervened with Mark.

The way he'd taken care of Glen the past few days.

He gave you everything back…why can't you believe you gave him something back as well?

When he found himself getting up and packing, he realized he just had.

After ten minutes, he had the phone out, called in a favor. While he waited for his friend to drop off his truck with the plow, he showered, then packed rapidly. The last thing he packed was the present he'd bought for Derek on his last mission, and headed over to Derek's house in his borrowed truck.

He'd caught him just in time, because Derek's front door was open, a large duffel waiting, the truck on and warming. Sometimes, leaving it in fate's hands was the best thing, Glen decided. And tonight, fate won.

He beeped twice and got out of the car. Derek met him on the porch as the soft snow fell around them.

"What are you doing here?"

Glen nodded back toward the truck. "I can get you through." "You don't have to do that."

"You stayed behind for me and missed your flight." "I did

that because I wanted to," Derek said.

"And I'm doing this for the same reason. Don't make me put you over my shoulder and drag you out of here."

"You and what army?"

"Fuck the Army. Navy does just fine on its own." Before Derek could react, Glen had him over his shoulder and was walking to the truck.

Derek was strong but he'd always known Glen was stronger, in so many ways.

When Glen put him down on the ground by the passenger's side, Derek pulled Glen to him in a hard kiss. Glen responded instantly.

"I'll let you drive me if you spend the holiday with me." Glen didn't answer so Derek continued. "What—you'll drive me there and turn right around?"

"I'm not good with family."

"You're not good with your family. Give mine a try," Derek implored, his hand still on the back of Glen's neck, same as it was that first night they'd met. Except this time, Glen was so much farther along. "Please, baby—I'd never do anything to hurt you."

"Please let me drive you. Not because it's tit for tat. But because I want to do it for you. You're exhausted from taking care of me. I'd never forgive myself if something happened to you," Glen said, and Derek conceded, because that step was already huge.

"Let me grab my bag and lock up."

The weather was terrible—even with the truck and chains and plow, it was a white-knuckle trip, but hell, that was Glen's specialty. Pulling it out of the fire— or ice as the case may be.

Derek tried to fight sleep and lost, curled up in the seat next to him and passed out for hours while Glen blasted his way through state after state.

The house was all white-picket-fence perfect, the way Glen's had once been. It reeked of happiness, but Glen especially knew that the outside was always a facade, could never be as good as it looked.

Except...he looked at Derek. This man was as good. Glen knew that with his heart and soul, and he was so tired of fighting himself.

"Hey, we're here."

Derek shifted. "Shit, you're like Superman."

"Quite a compliment coming from a Marine."

Derek laughed, then stared between the house and Glen. When he spoke, it was with a sudden seriousness that caught Glen off guard. "When we get home, move in with me."

"You dated someone for years and you weren't ready. We've known each other a couple of months and—"

"And it's right. No matter if you spend Christmas with me this year—or you never do—I can respect that. But I still want you to come home to me. I'll always make sure you're okay when you're with me."

"I believe you." He really did, with a feeling of trust that settled in his bones for the first time in what felt like forever. He leaned across the center console and kissed Derek, who didn't seem worried that his mom might see them. Derek put a hand on the back of his neck and tugged Glen in closer.

When they both pulled back, reluctantly, Derek told him, "Good. Then don't answer me right now. Think about it. Because I'm too damned impatient not to ask again, and soon."

"Could you be more bossy?" Glen asked. "Yeah, I can. And you'll love it."

Glen fought a moan, because he wanted nothing more than Derek to show him, right here and now. But it was neither the time nor the place for that. And his head was already swimming with contemplating Derek's offer.

The man was completely serious. And he was staring at Glen like he knew what he was thinking, so Glen told him, "Let's get our stuff out of the back."

"Our stuff?"

Glen nodded, and Derek didn't make a huge deal about it, just acted like that had always been the plan. Together, they waded through the knee-deep snow, the icy hail pummeling them as they walked.

Glen didn't feel a damned thing—between his happiness and his nerves—he was shot.

Derek's mother was waiting at the door. "I can't believe you made it through."

Glen watched as she hugged Derek tight. When they pulled apart, she held out her hand. "Alice Mann—so nice to meet you, Glen."

He shook her hand. "You too. Thanks for having me here."

"Any friend of Derek's," she said with a warmth that couldn't be faked. And then Derek's sister, Melissa, came into the hall and threw her arms around Derek and hugged Glen too, whether he wanted to be hugged or not.

"Sorry," Derek mouthed with a shrug, but Glen was all right. More so than he'd thought he'd be.

"You must be exhausted, driving all night," Alice said. "Go get some rest and I'll have food ready when you're done."

Glen had almost forgotten that somewhere along the road, it had turned into Christmas.

Derek led them up to the third floor—an open, loft-like attic room with a big bed and plush rug. It was warm, despite the hail slamming the windows.

"I want to tell you how much this means to me, but I'd rather show you," Derek murmured.

He relaxed in Derek's arms. Let the man fuss over him. Then he let Derek tie his arms down tight to the headboard and make love to him quietly.

10

Glen let Derek sleep, got up and showered and let the smell of food guide him downstairs. He steeled himself—for what, he wasn't sure, and he padded into the kitchen.

Alice was checking something in the oven, turned when she saw him. "Hope you got some rest."

"I did—thanks."

The lights flickered, and she looked up at them like she could will them to stay on. "We've been lucky so far. As long as this roast cooks, I'll be happy. But you must be hungry—sit and I'll get you something to snack on."

He wasn't about to argue—it had been a while since he'd eaten. She poured some hot chocolate into a mug, passed it to him and he drank the sweet concoction, calmer inside than he thought he would be.

She sat across from him with her own mug. "Thank you for getting Derek through this storm. It means more to me than you could possibly know."

"Yeah, well, he's done a lot for me," he said quietly.

"You've done a lot for him." There was pride and acceptance

in her tone and Glen's shoulders relaxed.

She was nice, but she wasn't pushing him to the point where he wanted to run. Instead, she plied him with cookies, like she knew sweets were his weakness, and then she showed him photo albums of Derek. As the lights flickered and the winds howled, Glen kept her calm during the storm, reassured her that the roast would be fine, even though he knew nothing about cooking.

Derek watched Glen sitting at the table with Mom, drinking cocoa and paging through photo albums.

He'd advised his mom to go slowly—she wouldn't have called Glen down here like this.

No, while Derek was sleeping, Glen had come down here purposefully. His chest squeezed as he backed slowly away, not wanting to interrupt their moment. Instead, he joined his sister in the living room, where she was putting the finishing touches on the tree.

Derek was usually here to help them pick it out on Christmas Eve. But Melissa had somehow managed to do so herself.

"I like him," she said, without being asked. "And you know I don't like everyone."

"Yes, I know. Speaking of..."

"Tommy and I are still together. He's with his family this year," she said with a dramatic sigh. "Mom's so happy you made it home."

"So am I." He was happy for a lot of things. He'd let go of a hell of a lot— Glen had as well. And they had a lot to show for it. Didn't matter the length of time—right was right.

"I like seeing your smile again," Melissa told him, gave him a quick peck on the cheek.

"Me too, sis…me too."

Later that night, after Merry Christmases had been said and the roast and potatoes and everything else in between had been eaten, the storm finally eased up. Glen and Derek were curled together in the attic guest room.

"Why is this easy?" Glen asked himself out loud.

"You're not easy—neither am I. But it's right," Derek said. "I think, in order to have or appreciate the very best, you have to go through the very worst. Living your life always looking to be on an even keel is safe, but it's boring."

"So you have to suffer to be really happy," Glen mused. "Like you don't know what it really feels like until you feel really shitty."

"Yeah, like that. It's a good time of year for miracles." "I'll take them every time."

Derek moved to open the bedside table drawer. "I wanted to give you this in private."

It was wrapped, and when Glen opened it, two keys fell out. "So this wasn't an impulse move-in-with-me discussion."

"No. I've known for a couple of weeks. Needed to find the

right time—and last night felt like it."

"It's pretty perfect," he said, took a minute to connect them to his own key ring. And then he said, "I've got something for you too."

He rifled through his bag and pulled out the unwrapped gift and handed it to Derek. He'd picked up the carved ebony statue—two figures symbolically twined to make one—on his last mission to Africa. It reminded him of everything he wanted with Derek. Made him think that it wasn't too late to go home and fix what he'd fucked up.

And he'd been right. "I bought it before I got sick. After I picked that fight…" He stared at the ceiling, shook his head. "God, I kept fighting, fucking things up. And they still worked out."

Derek smiled. Put the statue next to him on the night table and kissed him. "It's really perfect."

"Like you."

Derek snorted. "Remember you said that the next time you're pissed at me." "I'll try."

"You all right?"

He was. The family stuff would probably always overwhelm him but being accepted into the fold was comforting. There were no hidden agendas here—no snide comments. Just love.

Derek had been right—accepting himself was always going to be the hardest part. "Do I get to sit on Santa's lap?"

"Fuck Santa. You'll sit on mine." "That's a better offer." Glen smiled.

"For right now, it's all damned good." Derek paused, wondered if he should press his luck. "If you move in with me, that would be the best present ever."

Glen whistled softly. "You said you'd ask again soon, but man, you're fast." "I know what I want."

"You're lucky I like fast."

"I've been lucky ever since you walked into the bar." Derek meant that more than he ever thought he could.

"I want to be with you, Derek. Want to move in with you. I just can't believe…"

"Believe what?' Derek prompted softly when Glen paused for too long. "Can't believe you want to move in with me."

Derek kissed him fiercely, letting him know that, yes, that's exactly what he wanted. Let Glen know that it was all for real. And when they pulled apart for a second, Glen nuzzled his head against Derek's shoulder.

"Yes," Glen said finally. "In case I wasn't clear—yes."

"Baby, you just made my year." Derek stroked the side of Glen's face when the boy moved his head to look him in the eye.

"Love you," Glen said. "Not sure if it's too early to say it, but that's what I feel."

Derek held him. "Love you. Never too early."

"Fucking Christmas," Glen muttered, the lights burning softly across his face. He knew he'd celebrate it happily every year from now on. And he had Derek Mann to thank for it. For everything.

NEWSLETTER

Sign up for the newsletter of SE Jakes and her alter-ego Stephanie Tyler!

Be among the first to learn not only about new and upcoming books but also appearances and signings as well as special promotions and giveaways!

http://stephanietyler.com/newsletter/

HOLD THE LINE

INKED 1

Holding on loosely has never been such a challenge...

What happens when a tattoo artist and a Delta Force soldier keep a promise and take a cross-country trip together? Quinn and Con are about to finally meet and find out. Quinn thinks he's the responsible one, but he quickly learns that he needs to loosen up if he's got any shot of holding onto Con.

CHAPTER 1

Quinn McKenna glanced down at the stack of paper that had arrived certified mail just hours before, care of his younger brother, and then back up at the man hanging out by the pool table.

He didn't have a picture of Conlan "Con" Jenkins in his packet—just a basic description—but he realized now he'd have known the tall, handsome Delta Force soldier anywhere. There was something in his bearing that Quinn picked out easily. Maybe it was because Quinn's father and brothers had been Delta too, so he was in tune with the way they operated. Most of the Special Forces soldiers he'd come in contact with in his younger days, including his father and his brothers, appeared so outwardly casual to the rest of the world, blending in when they needed to. But Quinn knew that Con was consistently on alert, and that, if asked, he'd be able to give a description of every single person in the place tonight.

Bet you'll find him playing pool, Scott had also offered next to the name of the bar/restaurant picked for the initial meet-up, then added, *He'll be the one winning, with a lot of pissed-off guys around him.*

So yes, Quinn'd picked Con almost from the start, but remained at his table, casually scoping the soldier out while he ate dinner. He noted both he and Con were early for their meet-up, and wondered if they'd both been trying to outmaneuver the other. Not that there was any reason for that kind of thing—this was supposed to be a fun trip, not a competition. A trip ordered by Scott, and something neither Quinn nor Con could—or would—refuse.

Quinn could hear that phone conversation echoing in his ears.

"Bring my best friend to me," Scott had ordered him three weeks ago on the phone, and in Con's paperwork, Quinn now saw that Scott had written, *Bring my brother home to me.*

When they'd spoken on the phone weeks earlier, Scott had also explained, "Con's dangerous with too much time on his hands."

Quinn remembered wanting to bang his head against the wall but had asked instead, "How dangerous?"

"You'll travel with him for a couple of weeks—you tell me."

Quinn immediately understood just what his brother meant, because Con was obviously well versed at hustling pool. The guys he'd been playing had gone from friendly to very disgruntled, and Con either noticed and didn't give a shit or else he was oblivious.

Quinn was betting on the former.

Then again, Con had refused the bets at least six times, had told the men asking that it wouldn't be fair, and not in a cocky, assholeish way. But the men weren't listening and Quinn knew there was a fight in Con's future. And that meant there'd be a fight in Quinn's as well.

There was still time to bail. He glanced at his watch, noting he was still early enough that Con wouldn't miss him if he left. Unless Con had pegged him from the moment he'd walked in.

Scott wants this, he reminded himself. And he wouldn't refuse his brother, no matter how badly he wanted to.

And he really wanted to. But Scott couldn't make this trip this year, not like he'd planned, and so he'd asked Quinn and Con to do it in his stead. They'd start here, outside of L.A. and end up in the Catskills, and ultimately, Scott's wedding, by way of the strange and varied path Scott had created for them.

By rights, Scott should've been here, a buffer between them, the glue that would bond them. Con and Scott had served together. Sat on the bus together to Basic, and from that point forward they'd been inseparable. Con did come home with Scott for some holidays, but Quinn hadn't been there for any of those. He was the older brother, off sowing his wild oats, which was true. But during that time, he'd also become a licensed tattoo artist. He'd also been featured on a few of those ink shows on reality TV, but he had no real aspirations to be a regular, even though his boss wanted him to be. Mainly because the producers also wanted to include more about his personal life, thinking that would make for great TV.

But this wasn't TV—this was his motherfucking life, as he'd pointed out. His private life was private for a reason, although he'd never made any bones about his sexual orientation, or his bent toward BDSM. The writers of the show offered to find him love, especially if they could follow him into the club scene.

His boss at the tattoo shop told him he'd cave sooner than later. Right before he'd given Quinn the time off to make this road trip. And if that was a bribe, it was a pretty effective one. So he'd pushed back appointments. But really, Scott did the rest of the work, from the big things like booking hotels and restaurants to the mundane of actually planning the route ("*Con will tend to ramble and he doesn't like to use maps— says he doesn't need them*")—and yeah, that was so *not* how Quinn operated.

But hell, he couldn't deny how handsome Con was. Not pretty boy, no. He was rugged looking, lanky with a swagger that probably made most guys want to be him or fall to their knees and beg to be fucked by him.

It made Quinn want to push Con to his knees and force his cock in between those full lips, watch them swell from sucking as his eyes glazed with pleasure.

You're supposed to be keeping an eye on him, not fucking him.

Did Scott even know if Con was gay, or bi? Did it matter?

What mattered was that this would be the longest trip of Quinn's life.

As soon as Con saw the pool table, he'd known he was fucked. Because he was nervous. Jumpy. And as much as playing pool always got him in shitloads of trouble, it also calmed him.

He'd come back to California forty-eight hours earlier after eight months OUTCONUS. He'd routed through his home post for seventy-two hours and then he'd literally come straight to this bar in Normalsville, USA.

He wasn't ready in any way, shape or form to be around civilians. Scott knew that—it was probably why he'd given Con a chaperone, in the form of Quinn McKenna.

Quinn'd arrived ten minutes after Con. Situational awareness was his job, and a guy like Quinn caught his attention easily. He'd seen pictures, but none had done Quinn justice. He'd walked in like he owned the place.

And he's bossy as fuck, Scott had told him often. And the way Quinn'd marched in, like he was planning on taking and conquering, made Con smile. Mainly because he didn't play by bossy rules. But looking at Quinn...maybe he should start.

Still, Con had been ignoring him for the better part of an hour, in favor of racking up. The pool cue, the chalk, the sharp snick of the balls as they snapped smartly together all drew him in, especially because of the way they mixed with the smell of beer and tobacco and cologne, all the bar chatter and music. The familiar sounds of his childhood.

And the people...he could group them easily, had been born and bred to group them in the most advantageous way possible. The monied set. The good ole boys. The cowards. The troublemakers.

Where Quinn fit in, Con had some idea, but he was open to really finding out. After a few games. And so he'd shot several, fucking up the first break the way he always did. His dad thought that Con had just perfected the art of the scam easily. Con had let him think it.

What was the alternative? *No, Dad. I really didn't fuck up my games on purpose—I let my nerves get the best of me...*

"You had a clear shot. Blind man could've made it."

Con didn't bother glancing up at the sound of the voice. Guaranteed, it was a plaid-shirted guy who'd been sitting at four o'clock, trying to pin him down for a so-called friendly game of pool.

Right now, Con screamed "easy betting money." But Con didn't want to bet on pool, hadn't planned on hustling tonight. The pressure had started from Plaid Shirt and then a few of his friends, and Con suggested they keep it friendly, play for beers. But the guys thought he was chicken. Goaded him.

Finally, because he needed to play pool and make them shut the fuck up, he took the bet. He figured he'd given them enough of an out that he didn't have to feel guilty. Now, an hour later, he was up two grand and up against three pissed-off regulars who would no doubt try to roll him in the parking lot when he left. At this point, they were in the "refusing to let him leave" stage of bargaining. The "just one more game" bullshit, like they'd suddenly get lucky.

Ain't happenin', boys.

Finally, Quinn'd sidled up to the table, looking like just another guy checking out the action. But he wasn't just another guy—he was big and tall and handsome…and he turned a lot of heads. He could probably fight well. But really, Con wouldn't have any problem taking on these guys the way he took their money. He'd told them not to—he'd been truthful, so that absolved him of any guilt he might've had.

Hell, he had enough guilt already—needed a fucking U-Haul for it—and wasn't looking to add more weight to pull.

Instead, he took a drink of the seltzer water that'd been fueling him most of the night and finally made eye contact with Quinn. The two of them were standing slightly away from the pool table, watching Plaid Shirt rack up—again—with the others watching him like they were afraid he'd just disappear into thin air.

Con could definitely do that, but it was more smoke and mirrors than anything. All of this was. So he stared at the big man who looked at him, disapproval written all over his face. It was literally going to be like being watched by Big Brother. Although he looked nothing like Scott, Scott had shared family pictures ad nauseam.

Con had none. In return for warm fuzzy family pictures and their accompanying stories (that Con had actually liked but would never come right out and admit to), Con taught Scott to hustle pool. Well, to assist. Hustling was a skill best learned young and used regularly, especially when someone was depending on it for survival. He'd learned early on that if he didn't hustle, he didn't eat. That's how he'd grown up.

"You're good," Quinn said in a low, deep voice.

"I know," he said irritably as Quinn's dark eyes locked him in place. He swallowed, forced himself to look away.

"How long are you going to keep this up?"

"I've been trying to get out of here for an hour."

"So go."

"Gotta give them a chance to make their money back. Wouldn't be fair otherwise," Con pointed out.

"Since when's what you do fair?"

Con smirked. "Since now. And you have no idea what I do."

"Hustler with a conscience. Interesting."

Yeah, it was interesting all right. "I'll meet you two exits down the highway."

Quinn raised a brow but didn't say anything.

Con wanted to be annoyed, but he was too busy noticing the tattoos that snaked out from under Quinn's pushed-up shirtsleeves, and one that twined elegantly along the side of Quinn's neck. "Seriously. Don't wait here for me. I'll be fine. Trust me."

Quinn looked between Con and the pool table and gave a soft snort in retort.

Quinn didn't listen to Con's orders, mainly because he didn't take them, not that he didn't believe Con could handle himself. When Con readied to leave, Quinn saw three of the men follow him out. Quinn brought up the rear, walked out onto the dark sidewalk in time to see Con smoothly dispatching the three men, doing barely any damage, but enough to make the men go back inside the bar.

For reinforcements, Quinn figured.

"Ready?" Con called as he got on his Harley, which was parked two spaces over from Quinn's big truck.

"Do we have a choice?" Quinn asked as he started his truck.

Con laughed, a sound that carried over the roar of his own bike. "Unless you want to deal with more of them. I'm happy to do it."

Fuck. Not especially. Was it going to be like this for the entire trip, getting Con's ass out of scrapes?

"You weren't supposed to wait," Con called to him, right before he pulled out into the road. Quinn followed close behind, the two vehicles taking off smoothly into the night and disappearing without anyone following them.

They'd gotten lucky. Quinn knew that. He could only imagine the amount of times a trail of cars had followed Con.

Finally, he pulled off the exit, behind Con, as planned. They parked along the side of the rest stop where they'd have a good view if anyone drove in. It was mainly truckers stopping here this time of night anyway.

Con got off the bike and strolled up to Quinn's truck. Quinn opened the door and slid down to meet him. "What would you do if I wasn't here?"

Con laughed, sounding slightly crazy "What? You think I need you to bodyguard me? Newsflash—I don't."

"Fine. So we ride together and go our separate ways at night. You can hustle pool and defend your own honor."

"While you rest your old man bones? Sounds good."

"Let's leave my bone out of it," Quinn growled. Con looked right between his legs, letting his gaze linger, then slowly let it drift up to Quinn's face.

God, this fucker needed to be taught a lesson and Quinn was itching to do that, wanted to take him over his lap and...

Con grinned, like he knew what Quinn was thinking.

Which wasn't possible. He was military, not psychic.

"We're not doing that every night," Quinn informed him.

"Last I looked, this wasn't a military base and you aren't in charge of me," Con told him.

Quinn raised a brow. "You're looking for someone to take charge?"

Con hesitated for only the briefest second. "Did I say that?"

Well, he might as well have, because dammit, Con was screaming for someone—the right someone—to hold him down and fuck him.

But he was supposed to simply be taking a road trip to see Scott. With Con. "Escorting him," was how Scott termed it. As he put it, "Without you, Con would eventually make it here, probably with a police car in tow."

Quinn glanced at Con. "Doesn't the military have rules?"

"Lots of them. Be specific."

"Moral ones? Propriety."

Con snorted. Motioned to himself. "Not in uniform, right? And I don't see any MPs around. Dude, I'm free. And you're killing my buzz."

Quinn's buzz was nonexistent, unless he counted the low-level buzz in his head that made him want to strangle Con and take him in hand in equal parts, and *fuck*, that wasn't good.

Instead, he went back to the truck, grabbed the itinerary that was Con's and handed it to him.

Con began to flip through it, standing under the lights of

the Arby's in back of him. "Looks like our tour guide/travel agent took care of everything."

"Yeah, these came this morning." Quinn had glanced through the itinerary briefly. "It's got both weeks planned, down to the hotels he's reserved and paid for."

Con sighed and stuffed the folder in his bag. "Are we set for tonight?"

"Hotel's an hour away."

"We're starting tonight?"

"According to Mr. Control Freak, yes." He glanced at Con's bike. "Want to stow this? I've got a cover for it."

"You ride?"

"S'why I bought this truck." He opened the flatbed and pulled the ramp down. Con wheeled the bike up easily, chained it in and covered it up.

Then he joined Quinn in the cab, sliding into the passenger's side and dumping his camouflage duffel behind the seat. "She ride well?"

"Not bad. Better since I played with her."

"Gearheads," Con muttered, but he nodded with a smile when Quinn started the motor and it rumbled to life with a resounding roar.

Neither one of them was very talkative. They were both wound up from that last minute burst of adrenaline, and Quinn just wanted to get to the hotel before he lost that charge. With the radio pulsing some old school heavy metal—music Con didn't object to—Quinn tried to figure out the suddenly compliant soldier sitting next to him.

Scott'd never mentioned Con being gay or bi and it was obviously possible that he'd had no idea. Between DADT—because repealed or not it'd still been a part of Con's military life at one point—and the fact that these men were in one of the most gay-unfriendly professions, Quinn couldn't blame Con for not discussing his personal life.

Con didn't seem like he was the type to hide what he was, though. At least not off-base. While he could easily pass for straight, Quinn noted that, at least tonight, Con had made sure to catch as many men's eyes as he could.

Granted, Quinn had never come out and told Scott he was gay. He figured his family hadn't been able to handle the fact that he wasn't enlisting, and being gay would throw them over the edge. It wasn't a reveal he deemed necessary.

And the Dom part? Yeah, no fucking way.

Maybe he'd read Con's vibe wrong but, but…yeah, no. Especially not when Con had given him that smile and boldly looked him up and down.

Hell, had Scott known about him and told Con? Was this some kind of weird set-up?

Granted, if it was, Con had seemed as clueless about it as Quinn'd been. At some point, Con had started looking through the itinerary again. "Christ, he turned this into a military op."

"That he did."

"Well, this is what he wanted. Can't not comply with his

wishes now," Con pointed out.

Two weeks. "Think we can make it in one?"

"And hit all the hotspots he highlighted?" Con shook his head. "What's the rush? I'm making the most of this—I plan to have fun in as many states as I can."

Jesus. Quinn rubbed his forehead. Nothing about this trip was fun, especially the endpoint. There was still time to say "fuck it," to get on a plane and show up, and hell, what was Scott going to do? Send him back to gather up Con? The guy was a grown fucking man in the Army, for Christsakes—he could get himself across the country.

And if he couldn't? Well, then maybe Con had bigger problems than Quinn should be expected to handle.

By the time Quinn pulled the truck into the hotel's lot, it was close to three in the morning. Con let him check them in, take the keys, sign for the room, and then Con followed him into the elevator.

The room was a two-bedroom suite. Con walked toward the room to the left immediately.

"We'll sleep in today and travel through late afternoon. We'll get to the next stop before nine tomorrow night and we'll be back on Scott's schedule," Quinn said firmly. Con grunted, went through the connecting doors ("Without shared suites you'll never keep track of him," were Scott's instructions) and left the door open.

Quinn glanced into Con's room and saw the man's clothes in a trail leading to the bed. And Con was only under the sheet—really, only partially under—and very obviously naked.

And there was no ink on his body at all—at least from what Quinn could see, which was three quarters of a solid body. That was a shame, because Con really had the perfect contours.

Stop thinking about his contours, Quinn.

But he couldn't stop. These next weeks would no doubt be a crash course in everything Con. And what an education it would be, if tonight was any indication.

And since his mind was racing, he did what he always did when he needed to calm the fuck down—he sketched.

He'd been born with art in his blood, and he'd been sketching from the time he could hold a pencil. He'd also liked giving orders. "Bossy as fuck," his father would say. "He'll make a good general."

He glanced back and forth between the bed and the paper in front of him, drawing freehand…and feeling oddly freer than he had in a long damned time.

NOW AVAILABLE:

BOUND
BY
HONOR

MEN OF HONOR

TURN THE PAGE TO READ MORE...

MEN OF HONOR, BOOK 1

A promise forces two men to bare themselves... completely.

One year ago on a mission gone wrong, Tanner James failed to save the life of Jesse, his Army Ranger teammate. Before dying in that South American jungle, Jesse extracted a promise that won't let Tanner rest until it's fulfilled—no matter what it costs him.

Damon Price loved Jesse, but problems in their relationship had come to a head right before Jesse left on his final mission. Now a reluctant Dom and a man still in mourning, he's not happy when Tanner appears at his BDSM club. And even less happy with Jesse's last request—that Tanner sub for him for one night.

After a rough start, Damon realizes that the tough soldier, despite his protests, aches for someone to take control. And Tanner senses a hesitance, an insecurity in Damon that makes him wonder if he's simply a placeholder for Jesse, or if their tentative connection could grow into something more.

For Jesse's sake, they agree to try one weekend together. Then duty calls, and a series of attacks that have been happening near the club hits too close to home, making both men wonder if giving their hearts is a maneuver fraught with too much risk...

Warning: Contains rough language, rougher sex and warriors who fall hard for each other.

1

Tanner James had been to hell and back more times than he could count over the course of his twenty- six years and was always pretty sure he'd live to make the trip again. But this time, even as adrenaline raced through his body and every muscle tensed for battle, hell beckoned with a one-way ticket and without a goddamned firefight in sight.

No, that would've been easier, *much* easier than this slow crawl to the door of Crave—a BDSM club with the reputation of being both accessible and safe—the week before Christmas.

He looked up at the dark sign with white lettering at the entrance and thought about turning back and going home.

If he hadn't promised Jesse that he'd do this, that he'd look up Jesse's former boyfriend, he'd be home right now, having just returned from a month-long mission, not about to offer himself up like some bondage sacrifice.

This wasn't his scene. Not really. He was all about rough sex, was bisexual with a definite preference to men for as long as he could remember, used to having to *don't ask, don't tell,* thanks to his military career—but this? Having to go in and greet the owner with a message from his dead lover? Well, that was fucking weird and could get him thrown out on his ass.

Jesus Christ, this was going to suck.

The man checking patrons who entered was dressed in bright, loud colors. Tight black leather pants. Guyliner. And he flirted in an over-the-top manner with anyone he deemed hot enough.

Tanner knew he'd be the subject of the man's flirtation. Although he'd shrugged it off his entire life, the looks and stares and come-ons he'd been on the receiving end of forever told him he was handsome.

He was more interested in being the best Army Ranger he could, spent most days knee-deep in jungle crap with paint on his face and men who only cared that he could shoot an M-14 with dizzying accuracy.

"Hey."

"Hello, gorgeous. Please tell me you're alone." The man peeked behind Tanner, saw no one and clapped his hands. "Alone. There is a God."

"I'm looking for Damon Price."

"I'll bet you are," the man said with a shake of his head. "Shame, really, that they all want what they can't have."

"I just need to talk to him."

The man erupted into peals of girlish laughter and Tanner rolled his eyes. He'd never been into queens and this was why. If he was going to fuck a man, he was going to fuck a man. "Tell him I've got a message from Jesse."

The man stopped, nearly choked, but before he could answer, he was elbowed out of the way by a much taller blond man—ruggedly handsome although unsmiling, and Tanner wondered if he was face to face with Damon himself.

But rather than introduce himself, he asked, "What did you say about Jesse?"

"You heard me," Tanner bit out.

The man nodded slowly. "I heard you. I just don't know how Damon's going to feel about this." He paused. "Are you sure you want to go there?"

Tanner reacted before he could stop himself. "Why the *fuck* would you care where I want to go?"

The man raised a brow and held up a finger, indicating for Tanner to wait a minute, before disappearing down a back hallway.

Last chance to head for the hills. And despite the ease with which he could do so, Tanner remained rooted in place.

He couldn't see very far into the club at all from where he stood—it was designed purposely to let the incoming patrons hear the familiar sounds of sex occasionally rising over the music. The smell of sex was also unmistakable, partially hidden and mixed with whiskey and smoke. It was meant to beckon, to lead men astray…and Tanner didn't bother to hide his hard-on.

A few minutes later, Tanner was being led by the blond man who introduced himself as LC back to a private office with a big *Do Not Disturb* sign on the door.

No doubt, *this* counted as disturbing Damon, but it had been eating away at Tanner for a year now. He had to rid himself of this burden, do what Jesse asked and then go home and pretend none of it ever happened.

Before going in, he glanced at his watch. Just after midnight. Exactly the way Jesse had wanted it.

A hard growl of a voice called, "Come in."

LC stared at him, and Tanner, in turn, stared at the floor for a long moment. And then he opened the door and realized he'd been anything but prepared for Damon Price. Tanner was big and broad and strong, stood six foot three and turned heads wherever he went. But Damon—he was well over six foot five, with jet black hair and chiseled features. He stood, hands at his sides in a deceptively casual stance, dressed in full black leather and looking like a fucking badass.

Tanner nearly hyperventilated, because Jesse hadn't mentioned this part.

"He's my boyfriend and he owns a club," was all Jesse said. *"He's strong—reminds me of you. He's a Dom."*

"I'm not a Dom."

"No. But you could probably use one. It would be the only kind of man who could handle you."

Jesse had closed his eyes then before Tanner could tell him he had no interest in being anyone's bottom boy. Because Jesse had been talking to him about boyfriends and Doms when he'd been dying, slowly and painfully in the middle of a jungle in South America where he and his Ranger team had been on a mission, and Tanner had been fucking helpless to stop it.

Fuck.

He shoved his hands in his pockets so Damon wouldn't see the fists he couldn't uncurl and hoped the pain didn't show in his eyes.

This was supposed to bring closure—to both Damon and Tanner. There was no way to break a promise to a dead man.

Damon studied him for a few minutes. Tanner wasn't the type to squirm and he wasn't about to start now. Finally, the man said, "I hear you have a message from Jesse. And I swear to Christ, if you're fucking with me, I'll put your head through the wall."

Tanner snorted in spite of himself. "Okay, sure. I'd like to see you try."

Damon pushed away from the desk and stood toe-to-toe with him. "Talk."

Talk. Yeah, like it was that easy. "Jesse told me to come here—to ask for you. To tell you that…" Fuck. He shifted, aware that the proximity of Damon was freaking him out. If he hadn't been Jesse's, Tanner might've made a move without a second thought.

As if he knew what he was thinking, Damon arched an eyebrow at him, his lip curled into a half sneer.

Fuck it all. "I'm supposed to tell you to have a session with me. Jesse wanted it that way." "A session?" Damon repeated.

"Yeah. I'm supposed to let you Dom me. It was Jesse's dying wish."

Damon paled, took a step back from Tanner, and then another. "Is this a sick joke?"

"Do I look like I'm joking?"

"You little fuck." Damon had Tanner's shirt bunched in his fists, was slamming him against the office wall hard. "You sick bastard. You think you can ingratiate yourself to me by using Jesse?"

Tanner ground his teeth together hard and tamped back his anger. He'd known Damon wouldn't take this well. If Tanner had been in the same position, he doubted he would either. "He asked me to wait a year before I came here. He died after midnight."

"How do you know that?" Damon demanded. "Even I don't know that."

No, he wouldn't. The mission was deemed classified—and Jesse's time of death a closely guarded secret. "I was with him when he died."

Damon let out a long, hissing breath and let go of Tanner's shirt.

"I'm sorry—I didn't know how else to tell you. Jesse made me promise—"

"Stop saying his name," Damon growled hoarsely.

"He made me promise I'd wait the year. Said you wouldn't be ready before that. That you'd need to be dragged back into the land of the living, kicking and screaming. He said to tell you…to use the skull- and-crossbones collar with the broken latch." He spoke fast, stopped to catch his breath at the end. Gauged Damon's reaction.

The man hadn't moved a muscle during Tanner's speech. Simply stared, and Tanner tensed more, wondering if he was going to have to fight tonight.

Fighting and fucking were definitely two of his favorite things to do, sometimes all in the same night—or hour—or hell, the same time, but he had a feeling that he'd be pushing his luck taking on this guy.

He was in way over his head. And he couldn't remember the last time—if ever—he'd felt that way.

Damon's features relaxed slightly. He sat back on the top of the desk, folded his arms and stared Tanner up and down. A hard, assessing stare that was enough to make Tanner hard with desire and anticipation.

He wasn't sure why the sudden thought of Damon taking him got him hot, but that was short-lived, because he saw the tension in Damon's stance, the pain in his eyes. Tanner wanted to apologize, but he wasn't sure what for. Wanted to tell Damon that he was scared to fucking death that the Domming would actually happen—and also scared that it wouldn't.

He was so fucked up he could barely see straight.

Damon finally spoke. "I wouldn't touch you. You're not man enough to handle me."

Jesse's words echoed in Tanner's ear. *It would be the only kind of man who could handle you.*

Tanner hadn't been able to handle a relationship—or being touched, really, since what happened to Jesse last year. And so he nodded and he said, "You're right about that. This was a mistake."

The failure hanging on him heavily, he pushed out the door, went through the club and headed for the parking lot.

Jesse.

Damon had mourned over that man, cried over him, beat his fists against the wall, up until three months earlier. Things had eased, but he still wore the cloak of grief that sometimes threatened to choke him.

Now was one of those times. He'd waited until the gorgeous man left his office before he fell apart and tried his best not to hyperventilate.

Use the skull-and-crossbones collar with the broken latch.

The boy who'd just left his office would have no way of knowing that—wouldn't have known that Damon kept that collar in his loft, had fixed the latch right after Jesse died because it was one of the only things he could do.

Damon wouldn't be able to use the damned collar on this boy—Jesse knew that collaring meant something—that it didn't happen on a first night together.

You don't even know the boy's name.

He shuddered involuntarily that he'd thought of him as *the boy*. Because that's what he'd called Jesse—and only Jesse.

Jesse had been the first to ever thaw what Damon had considered a heart of ice. First, and the *only*.

But something tugged at his gut.

He could've been lying. This could be part of an elaborate scam.

The only thing was, the man had definitely been military. A Ranger, like Jesse, or so he said. Damon didn't doubt it, had a nose for those things, having been in special forces himself what seemed like a lifetime ago. And the timing was exactly right. Jesse had died a year ago, nearly to the hour, although he'd lied to the boy about not having that information.

Fuck.

He called through the open office door, "LC, grab that guy who just left."

"I'm not your bitch," LC drawled, and no, LC was no one's bitch...not since Styx left. "And he's already in the lot."

"Dammit."

LC held his gaze for a second and then called to one of the bodyguards. "Renn—grab the guy in the brown leather jacket who just left. And bring a few guys—he won't come willingly."

LC didn't say anything more, didn't have to, and just headed to the front of the club to supervise. And Damon waited in his office, trying not to pace. Trying not to picture what the boy would look like, bound and spread for him.

Trying to pretend he wasn't hard at the thought of it.

He shifted but could do nothing to hide the erection in the pants he wore, and when LC barged back into the office, it was the first thing he noticed.

Thankfully, he didn't comment on it, just said, "They've got him and he's not happy."

"Makes two of us."

"Did he really know Jesse?"

Damon nodded. "He says that Jesse sent him here—wanted him to have a session with me."

LC's eyes widened, but wisely his mouth remained closed. He was part owner of Crave, working mainly behind the scenes. He was also Damon's best friend—the only person Damon confided everything in. The only one he trusted enough to let him run the business in those months after Jesse died, when Damon couldn't get out of bed most days. LC had finally gotten him up and functioning.

Just then, the boy was dragged back in by three men—he was pissed for sure, but not fighting as hard as he could. Damon knew that, and whether it was grief or curiosity or both, he couldn't tell yet.

"Let him go," Damon commanded, and the men dropped him and left the room with LC, the office door shutting behind them as the boy stumbled forward until Damon caught him, held him hard by the biceps and stared at him again.

He was handsome as hell—all-American-looking, a blond haired, blue-eyed devil, even with his lips twisted into an angry grimace.

"What the fuck do you think you're doing?" The boy jerked out of his grasp and yes, he was strong. Damon had suspected as much. Earlier, when Damon had him by the shirt, backed against the wall, he hadn't flinched. It was the calm of a man who knew how to fight—who knew how to kill.

"What's your name?"

A jut of a chin, a glint of wild eyes and he ground out, "Tanner."

"Why did you come here?"

"Because I made a promise to Jesse when he was dying. I don't break promises like that."

"And you're willing to follow through on what he wanted."

Tanner pressed his lips together—he wanted to say no, that much Damon knew. For some reason, this handsome, strong, brave man wanted nothing to do with being Dommed, and it didn't appear to be for the usual reasons.

No, he wasn't uncomfortable, either in this club or with Damon and his leathers. But something was most definitely wrong with him.

"I'll do what Jesse wanted, yes."

"But you don't think you're man enough."

He waited for Tanner to snap an answer back, but none came. Instead, he shrugged.

"Well then, there's no time like the present. But no collar." He motioned for Tanner to follow him, out the door of the office, down a small hallway and into a room marked Room

Four.

Once inside, Damon pressed a few buttons to bring the lights up and to remove the shading from the plate-glass divider that separated the room from the rest of the club.

As soon as he did so, the bar began to cheer. Damon activated the two-way speakers as well, so the sounds went from muffled to completely clear.

Tanner's eyes widened. "We're doing this here—where everyone can see?"

"Yes. That's what Jesse would've wanted."

Tanner couldn't have known that was the furthest thing from the truth—that Jesse understood the value of privacy at the start of a D/s relationship.

That Jesse would hate him for this.

Well, Damon hated Jesse for dying and leaving him. For refusing to quit the military and let Damon take care of him for the rest of his life.

For recognizing that Damon had been slowly dying inside during the last year of their relationship and continuing to satisfy his own needs instead.

Tanner swallowed hard and then he nodded.

Yes, let's see if this man is for real.

NOW AVAILABLE:

BOUND
BY LAW
MEN OF HONOR

TURN THE PAGE FOR A SNEAK PEEK...

MEN OF HONOR, BOOK 2

The one man he can't forget is the one whose memories could destroy them all.

After the one man he trusted disappeared, it took Law Connor ten years to take a chance on another relationship. Trouble is, right about the time he's finally ready to let go of the past, the past stages a hostile takeover.

Back when they were teens, Styx was the boy with no memory. He and Law had each other's backs until he was forced to leave to keep Law safe. Now a CIA agent, he's finally discovered who he is, and why he's a hunted man.

Detective Paulo McMannus has almost succeeded in helping Law forget his lost love when Styx comes plowing back into their lives. No way is Paulo giving up his lover without a fight.

Suddenly Law finds himself on the run with Styx, the man who can still bring him to his knees...and with Paulo, the man who brought him back to life. The worst part? He can't choose between them. And it's getting harder to remember why he should.

Warning: Contains rough language, rougher sex and warriors who fall hard for one another.

PROLOGUE

He'd been Styx for literally as long as he could remember.

If there was a birth certificate that proved otherwise, he'd yet to stumble on it. His reissued one gave a date of birth that seemed reasonable, since his old hospital records were simply gone—it was as if he'd materialized out of nowhere. Having absolutely no memory of his youth before the age of sixteen didn't help matters any. His first centered on waking up on a bench in Central Park, wandering into a gay club where he ended up crashing on a cot in the back for a while, until the owner invited him home.

The owner was Greg, who'd figured Styx for underage and had given him a refuge and a new life. The one who'd helped him get the new birth certificate and ID. At first, Styx had waited for the catch, assumed Greg wanted something from him. As it turned out, Greg did. He wanted Styx to grow up safe and sound, was paying it forward, the way a man had done for him years earlier.

Law had already been there about two years when Greg took Damon in, followed in swift succession by Styx. None of them were formally adopted by any means—CPS wouldn't have looked kindly on a forty-year-old gay man taking in underage gay boys, but it had been aboveboard from the start, a light in all three men's lives that ultimately saved them—from outside forces as well as themselves. It had been a real home—and Styx owed the man everything.

All three had been straddling the line between boy and man and had been drawn to Greg as if he were some sort of Guardian Angel. Styx had never changed his opinion of that.

Greg had never asked for a penny. He'd died about sixteen years ago and Styx still missed the hell out of him. Missed the other men as well. Styx had left them when he was almost twenty without so much as a note in the middle of the night when a threat from his past came out of the blue, and he turned himself in to the CIA a year later, when the burden of his past got too much to bear alone. For the past sixteen years, he'd lived like the spook he was.

He'd kept up with Law and Damon—both had gone the way of the military, and they remained friends, running clubs together up until a few months ago. He'd only allowed himself to visit Law three times, and although he'd never come right out and told Law or Damon what he was, both men had spent enough time around elite forces to be able to sniff out the fact that he was a spook.

It was what he did—who he was. And lately, it had him missing Law, the love of his damned life and the man he left behind, to the point where he was driving himself crazy.

But the past…it was coming for him again. Although he knew why, he still had yet to remember it for himself. And now, he had a chance to find out the full, fleshed-out version, and he was driving to reach the place where it would be delivered to him.

And so Styx walked up the stairs and closed the door, and he waited for the knock that would change his life.

LC slammed out of Crave, the BDSM club he used to be part owner of and where he never should've gone back to in the first place, got into his Porsche, and let it coast along the deserted streets. He willed himself to relax, let the music pound through him, but he knew that wouldn't work.

No, he needed to fuck. He'd already fought, slamming the shit out of some asshole who'd tried to throw his weight around at the club. And LC, already primed for action, had taken over, ignoring Damon telling him to stand down.

Damon, his friend and other former owner of the club, had yanked him off the man and hadn't said another word, and LC had left before he did or said something he'd regret.

He was so damned tired of regrets. Tired of being alone and thrashing around at night, dreaming of two different men—one he loved and one he was falling for.

Thing was, the past few weeks, the dreams had been… different. And it was time to start listening to where his subconscious was pushing him.

The houses flew by him and he knew where he had to go, the destination calling him like a beacon.

He headed up the walk and let himself in the main door, a skill he'd used widely and well for years, almost long forgotten, and it made him smile when he remembered it easily. The lock clicked open and he went up the three flights with stealth and thought about doing the same to the apartment door.

But he knocked instead, two hard bangs, and he heard movement inside. He hoped the man was alone, wanted him to be—needed him to be, even though he had no right to ask or expect that at all.

Where the hell have you been? was written all over his face, and the man refused to let LC in at first. But LC persisted and Paulo relented, and finally LC barreled in, grabbing and kissing the man until he stopped resisting and twined his hands in LC's hair and moaned into his mouth.

He practically carried the man back inside the apartment, kicked the door closed behind him before they tumbled to the floor, clothes ripping off, grunting, grabbing.

Then he pulled back. "I've been thinking about you. Dreaming about you…can't stop."

"About time," was all the other man said before LC covered his mouth again with a kiss.

The knock startled him, although it shouldn't have. Styx hesitated before opening the door—a highly trained, gun-carrying, wet-work assassin hesitated opening the damn door to his own apartment and yeah, maybe it was time to think about getting the hell out of Dodge.

But he opened it, the door to his past, took the envelope from the man's hands and didn't look him in the eye. His hands shook, making the fat envelope flutter in his fingers, the only sound in the otherwise silent room.

The world was silent at three in the morning, and typically, he liked that. Now, he longed for sounds, any sound but the tearing of the envelope and the unraveling of a life long buried by necessity.

He held that life in his hands, and the responsibility, the revelations, all threatened to crush him if he wasn't careful.

For the first time in a long time he realized he no longer wanted to be careful.

1

Paulo wasn't taking no for an answer, so LC had no choice but to concede to having dinner with the man. They were getting past the anonymous fucking stage and Paulo knew that, took advantage of him when he was weak from orgasms. Hence, the fancy goddamned dinner at an expensive restaurant where the detective obviously knew the staff. They got a private table in the back and appetizers began arriving without them having to place any orders. Paulo kept pouring the wine and LC got looser with each glass, and he knew he'd be going home with Paulo again that night for sure. Or maybe he'd take Paulo back to his new apartment for the first time, a new place, a fresh start…the same guy more than once, and that was a fucking record that had remained unbroken for ten years.

"Tell me what LC stands for," Paulo murmured now. "Or I'll tie you down and fuck it out of you."

"That's incentive to tell you?" LC asked as he scanned his menu for the main courses, not wanting to let Paulo see how turned on he got when Paulo spoke like that. Because he did so easily, his eyes hot, and LC remembered how good his body had felt against the younger man's.

Before last night, it had been about three months since he'd seen him last. Paulo had come to visit LC in the hospital after he'd thwarted an attacker who'd been hurting men outside Crave. Before that, Paulo had given him a gift—a gift certificate, to be exact, for a tattoo, which LC hadn't used yet. Paulo's torso was close to being covered with them, intricate designs that swirled over muscles in his back and arms and made him that much goddamned harder to resist.

LC loved looking at them, loved tracing them with his tongue, his fingers, watching the way they moved when LC was pounding him, the way he had last night.

"I was glad you came over," Paulo said after they'd finished the appetizers and waited on the next course.

LC had been surprised, too. He'd been restless for months and prowling the club scene no longer held his interest. Crave was sold and things were moving forward.

Everyone was moving forward and he'd been standing still. At first, there had been a lot to do with the sale of the club and the lofts and the construction of the new apartments he and Damon bought, along with the rest of the building. They were now living on opposite ends of the top floor, and the plan was to renovate and rent the rest of the apartments.

There was still a hell of a lot to do, but LC didn't feel like handling any of it, especially not last night. No, he'd wanted to handle someone, and his car had pointed in the direction of Paulo's place almost as if he'd had no control.

But LC knew that was bullshit.

Paulo had barely been able to get out a hello before LC had him pinned, telling Paulo he'd been dreaming about him before he could stop himself. After that, it was a blur of hands and tongues and *oh yeahs*, and then LC was agreeing to dinner, because he'd just taken the man without so much as a this-is-where-I've-been-for-the-past-few-months explanation.

He'd stayed through until the sun came up and straggled back to his new place, and now he was here, next to this man in this dark restaurant, and he'd been turned on from the time Paulo had picked him up.

If he was honest with himself, Paulo was handling him and LC really fucking liked it.

Paulo hadn't asked him any more about the dreams LC had about him, and for that, LC was grateful. Because this, the tug in the stomach when Paulo looked at him, was new… the first time since Styx, and he knew this man could make him happy, if he allowed it.

He downed the rest of his wine and stood before he told Paulo that. "Headed to the restroom—I'll be back."

"I'd join you, but I have a reputation in this place," Paulo said with a sly smile.

"I'm sure." LC threaded his way through the back hallway, found the men's room. He pissed and washed up in the private restroom, wiped his hands on a paper towel, and it was all normal. So normal.

Until the lights went out and shots rang out inside the restaurant and an arm came up across his body, a hand over his mouth, and his natural instinct to fight like hell was quelled with a single breath.

Styx. He'd recognize the man's scent—his touch—blindfolded. Many a time he'd actually done so, but this situation was a thousand percent different.

"Not a word." Styx's voice, rough like gravel. Rougher when he was angry or aroused. His breath was warm and minty—Altoids. The man had always been addicted to them.

Damn, you remembered the oddest things when your ass was on the line. And speaking of asses, his was pressed hard to Styx's groin…and the man's arousal was unmistakable. Nice to know he wasn't the only one affected by the close proximity.

He moved his head and Styx took his hand away.

"Paulo," he said, and Styx answered, "Your friend's safe—my associate has him."

Good, that was good, but Jesus, what was going on here?

He heard the slight snick of a gun's safety being released and then heavy footsteps. Whoever was coming wasn't interested in stealth.

Not good.

"Whatever happens, stay put in here. I'll take care of everything." Styx barely mouthed the words but LC heard them loud and clear. And then he was left alone in the dark, and yeah, that was the story of his goddamned life with and without Styx, and he listened and waited.

No more shots, but someone had been killed. LC had been around stealth and death long enough in the Army to the point where he could taste the violence. He'd been on the receiving end of it since birth.

Goddammit, LC, shake that shit off.

And then Styx was back, tugging at him, and LC resisted. "I'm not going anywhere until you tell me what the hell's going on out there."

"There's trouble. Now shut up and do what I say."

"I'm so beyond listening to you."

"You have no idea who and what you're up against. Come with me," Styx said, and LC reluctantly followed him into the restaurant's storeroom, close to the parking lot. And even though it was dark as night inside the restaurant's back room, LC would know the man, could practically see the dark blond hair, longer than it had been, eyes that never failed to mesmerize him, the hard body and even harder cock that had probed him earlier.

LC knew what he was up against—and he was powerless to stop it. And when he started to edge past Styx, Styx let him go at first and then pushed him hard against the wall by the door.

"Are you with that guy?" he whispered into LC's neck, and he wanted to tell Styx not to do that.

Instead, he ground out, "His name is Paulo. And now you're worried about my dating habits?"

"I'm always worried about you."

"The not calling or writing is a great way to show that."

"It's the way it has to be."

Has to be…not using the past tense meant that's what would happen after Styx did whatever it was he needed to here. "What, exactly, is happening out there to get the CIA involved?"

"Can't tell you."

"Right. I don't have the clearance to be involved in any part of your life." Never did. Never would. "Let fucking go of me."

"You can't leave now."

"Then you'll have to arrest me."

With that, Styx reached up and yanked LC's arms down and behind his back, and when the cuffs snicked on his wrists, he cursed bitterly. "Where's Paulo?"

"Safe."

"Not what I asked."

"Are you two serious?"

"Why don't you tell me? You've been spying on me for God knows how long."

"I call it keeping you safe."

"Get. The fuck. Off me."

Styx didn't listen. Never did, which was why the military hadn't been for him. "You bottom for him?"

"I'm trying to figure out why the hell you would care if I did."

"Guess I have my answer. And you know why."

"Not anymore, Styx. Too much time's passed."

He felt Styx's body stiffen, thought the man would release him. And then…

And then Styx's hand went to his cock as he sucked on the back of LC's neck along the spot—*that spot*—he'd discovered drove LC wild.

The only one who'd ever found it, and oh God, he was going to come in his fucking pants if Styx didn't stop.

And Styx would not stop.

"Like that, baby?" Styx whispered after licking the spot where LC knew there'd be a red mark that would stay there for days, then used his tongue and teeth and hands, slipped into LC's half unzipped jeans to work his magic.

"Fuck…please…don't, Styx." But he was saying *don't* and meant *don't stop*. And it was something he wanted— needed—too much to struggle more.

He'd always been a goddamned whore for this man—that would never change.

"Styx." The name, moaned into the dark, and if the man called him by his nickname, he'd lose it in his pants.

A few minutes and then a husky whisper answered, "Yeah, come right now, Law."

Law.

Law had no choice. His body always deferred to Styx's wishes. *Always.*

Styx wiped the man's stomach with some hastily grabbed napkins—he'd pulled Law's shirt up before he came so at least there wasn't a huge mess, and it had taken everything to not get on his knees and let Law come down his throat.

He threw the used napkins aside and fixed Law's clothes as the man remained silent, his breathing calming from the riot it had been moments earlier, when he'd come and cried out Styx's name.

God, he'd been dreaming about that for fucking ever.

"How long have you been checking up on me?" Law asked finally, his voice hoarse.

"Since the second I left your side."

"Right, and that was your damned choice." Law was furious. He slammed Styx off him and Styx hit the wall hard, and he tried to stumble forward.

Too late. Law had him pinned. Law, who had elite training and had gotten the handcuffs off like they'd been paper. Now, his body ground against Styx's. "You're a goddamned coward, running from me. From us."

"You don't understand."

"Then make me," Law demanded. When Styx said nothing, Law brought his mouth on Styx's in a punishing kiss meant to torment him with memories. His tongue forced itself into Styx's mouth, his cock pressed against Styx's as their groins ground together and finally, Styx brought his hand up to twist in Law's hair, keeping him from breaking the kiss. He tasted like Styx and mint and God, he'd missed this more than he even knew.

This was why he'd stayed away completely. For him, Law was like a drug—addicting and intoxicating, and he was in so much trouble.

He didn't care. Not when Law's hand reached between them and unzipped Styx's jeans so his hard cock slapped unfettered into Law's hand.

Styx groaned against his mouth at the contact, felt Law smile and then his hand stroked his cock in a way that Styx remembered, played with his Prince Albert piercing in a way that made Styx want to scream and fuck him immediately.

Law had always been talented. Now, more so and Styx wanted nothing more than to let him take over completely, to admit everything to him and beg for forgiveness.

He was this close to doing so, especially when Law stroked harder and fast and Styx's balls tightened and his orgasm loomed imminently.

"Fuck…Law." He threw his head back as his hips bucked uncontrollably.

Law could always make him come like this, could always make him lose control…and love it. Styx wondered if Law felt the same or if the loss of control would make Law angry and retreat back into his shell once the orgasm faded and he regained his senses.

Law didn't clean him or zip him, left Styx to do it himself and when he was done, the lights came up—Tomcat's signal for the all-clear. For now, at least.

The man's real name was Clint, but he hadn't used that in the year and a half he'd been on the sting inside the motorcycle gang's operation. Better that Styx and everyone else used the call sign. Better…and safer.

Law was staring at him, sizing him up. Goddamn, Law looked good. Rugged, sensual…age had done him well. "Law, you've got to let me explain."

"I know what you want. You want control over me. You don't want me, but you've made sure I can't be with anyone else." Law was furious, ten years of pent-up anger tearing into Styx's soul.

He couldn't admit to Law that he'd done it enough to himself. Oftentimes it made him seek escape in whiskey and men until he couldn't see straight. And it never goddamned helped worth a damn.

He reached out to pull Law close, to admit something when they heard more shots. And Styx did grab Law, but only to stop him from running through the restaurant to check on his friend. "Wait—stop," he told the man, and Law consented for a second as Styx called Tomcat.

Tomcat told him, "There's another assassin—get the hell out of there."

"It's okay—everyone's all right," he lied to Law. "We've got to get out of here."

Law leveled him with a gaze, his voice as dangerous as Styx had ever heard when he stated, "Not without Paulo."

When Paulo first heard the shots that rang out from the kitchen, he sprang into action. ID'd himself as a cop, told everyone in the restaurant to get down and stay down under tables or behind the bar and then he pulled his gun and snaked his way through the hallway toward the kitchen. Prayed that LC hadn't gotten caught in the crossfire.

He remained flat against the wall, ready to check the bathroom for LC when he caught sight of a tall man coming down the corridor, toting a gun and flashing his badge. CIA. He motioned for Paulo to duck into the small break room to his right, and he did.

"What's going on?" he asked the agent.

"We have it under control."

"My friend was in the bathroom—"

The agent held up his finger and spoke into the mic on his wrist, then asked, "You Paulo?"

"Yes."

"He's all right. He knows you're okay." He put his arm down and extended his hand. "Call me Tomcat. Nice work keeping everyone calm out there."

"Do you need me to call the precinct?"

"I'm sure they're coming—right now, we'd prefer to keep

this quiet."

Yeah, that was how the feds did things, but Paulo couldn't shake the feeling that the danger hadn't passed. That Tomcat was actually shielding him from something.

Was this man protecting him? "I don't need a bodyguard."

Tomcat simply grinned a little and murmured into the mic on his wrist again. The man was at least six foot-five, with dark hair, tattooed arms and a fierce-looking sawed-off shotgun. Looked like some kind of rogue agent. "You're gonna stay with me anyway."

Paulo didn't answer, and the men remained silent for what seemed like a hell of a long time. Then more shots rang out and he and Tomcat immediately went guns up against either side of the door.

"I'm going—you stay," Tomcat told him.

"Fuck that. What about all the people in the restaurant?"

"You're my concern."

Paulo nodded as if he conceded, because it was faster. Left the room a minute after Tomcat and went in the opposite direction toward the main part of the restaurant. He checked on the patrons, assuring them that he would protect them, making sure no one needed medical attention, because some of them looked like they were in shock.

And then he stilled, because it was too quiet and not at all like a typical aftermath. Whether or not Tomcat was after someone in the kitchen, there was more than one assailant here.

Paulo checked the windows of the restaurant—it was all quiet on the street front, but that wasn't odd. It was a dead-end, out-of-the-way place and the restaurant was the only destination. The parking lot was in the back and there was only one front entrance from the street.

But there was another doorway to the right—no doubt to a back staircase. Paulo saw the knob turn and then a man came barreling out from where he'd been lying in wait.

And he was staring right at Paulo. Gunning for him.

Paulo didn't wait to ask how long he'd been there, aimed and pulled the trigger twice, took the bastard down without hesitation.

He'd learned his lesson once, the hard way—hesitation cost you—and, if you were lucky, it was only your pride.

"It's okay," he told the patrons, went to the downed man with his gun still drawn, kicked the gun away from the body and knelt to take a pulse.

There was none. Paulo felt for his ID and pulled out a couple of photographs instead.

The first was a picture of him leaving the hospital, dated three months earlier, according to the back. The next showed LC in the hospital, sleeping in his bed, and a piece of paper had the name of the restaurant and the time of their reservation on it.

This had been an ordered hit.

The thought that he and LC were being targeted churned his stomach, and he continued to roust the dead man until

Tomcat was hauling him to his feet and sirens sounded in the background.

"Jesus, but you don't listen."

Paulo jerked out of his grasp and checked his cell phone, pulled out the battery and found no bugs, but that didn't matter—they could've triangulated the signal some other way. He turned it off just in case it was sending out a signal as Tomcat checked out the dead man on the floor.

"Please, help my husband."

Paulo turned immediately to help the older gentleman who was having trouble breathing. The air smelled like gunpowder and was thick with fear, and Paulo got the man flat with his feet up as his wife gave him his heart meds under his tongue.

In a minute, the man's color came back and Paulo allowed Tomcat to move him away.

"Where's LC?" he demanded as Tomcat waved the paramedics in to help. Two men in suits—more obvious agents than Tomcat—came in behind them, presumably to smooth over the situation.

"You're a pain in the goddamned ass," Tomcat muttered to him as they walked toward the kitchen. Paulo saw the blood spatter but he wanted to see LC for himself and that was more important than investigating right at the moment.

"Listen, cop—"

"Detective."

Tomcat stopped in the middle of the hallway. "Whatever.

Look, this is a bad situation."

"That guy was an assassin," Paulo said, and Tomcat stared at him as Paulo shoved the pictures into his hands. "He was gunning for me before I'd even turned around. My picture was in his goddamned pocket. Mine and LC's. So don't goddamned bullshit me anymore."

Tomcat put his hands up as if in surrender, told him, "I'm going to put you in the kitchen with your friend and another agent. Think you can stay put and stop being a hero long enough to get an explanation?"

Paulo stared at him, trying to determine if that was sarcasm, and saw nothing but respect in the man's eyes. It might make things easier, but this was far from over.

After Law refused to leave, there were two more shots that practically had him clawing at the door. He'd even tried to take Styx's gun to go out there but Styx held him back and listened on the mic as Tomcat kept him up to date.

Apparently, the cop was suddenly a hero—and completely fucked at the same time. He'd discovered the hit out on him and Law…the only thing he didn't know was that Styx was the main target.

If Styx had his way, no one beyond him and Tomcat would ever know that part. But it was far too late to keep the secret that his father was also after Law, and Paulo now, by default.

The only one he would keep was the fact that his father didn't want him back into the fold this time—no, the man wanted him dead.

"Where's Paulo? I want to see him," Law demanded.

"Fine." Styx gritted his teeth and muttered to Tomcat using the mic on his wrist. "Bring him in here."

It only took a minute before Tomcat was ushering Paulo in, the towheaded man looking more handsome than Styx remembered.

Paulo looked more than pissed, glared at Styx as he went to Law who was barreling toward him too. "You all right?"

The complete concern on both their parts was impossible to miss and threatened to overwhelm him, and he almost turned away when Law tugged Paulo into his arms, murmured, "Jesus, I'm fine. Heard the shots."

"Good." Paulo looked over Law's shoulder at Styx, his eyes held questions but he didn't say anything else.

"Can we get out of here and go home?" Law turned to ask Styx.

"No." Styx glanced at Tomcat who then slipped out of the room, no doubt to get the safe house directive in order, because what would happen next would not be pleasant for any of them. "These men are dangerous."

"And they're after us?" Law asked.

"They're after you because of me. They followed me to your hospital room and they've been tailing you ever since," Styx admitted.

"Why?" Law demanded, ignoring the part about the hospital visit, which made Styx's gut tighten. What had he expected, Law to run into his arms with that admission?

"Because they know that the best way to get to me is through someone I love."

Paulo stared between the two of them as he remained in Law's arms—because Law was holding on to him tightly. "You're the one who left him for years."

"You're the one who'll leave before the year's out, if your stay-in-one-place-for-two-years-or-less pattern holds. Or is Law the love of your life? The one who'll make you stay, even if it means trouble?"

Paulo turned back to Law. "At least now I know your first name. But that doesn't mean I don't get to tie you down."

Paulo almost smiled at the growl the blond man named Styx emitted after his comment about tying LC down.

Law. Granted, Paulo had known LC's real name was Lawrence Connor because he'd investigated his past—he'd just been waiting for LC to tell Paulo himself and it had killed him not to be able to use it. And that asshole CIA guy was probably the only one LC let call him that. So yeah, the pleasure at the zing was short-lived because he was the one getting screwed in this situation.

Law. It suited the handsome man whose hair was a darker blond than both his and Styx's.

He wasn't even touching Styx's comment regarding his past. Styx, who was glaring between him and Law, even as Law gave him a small grin. "It's a deal."

"I hate to interrupt this magic moment," Styx started, and Paulo broke away from Law, fisted his hands and went toe-to-toe with Styx. The agent was a few inches taller than he was, but Paulo had taken on bigger and badder in his time, and he wasn't going to let this motherfucker think Paulo would kowtow to him.

"Then don't."

"Got yourself a bodyguard, Law?" Styx asked with a grin Paulo itched to punch off his face.

Law stepped in between them, his hand on Paulo's shoulder, tugging him back even as Paulo demanded, "Why aren't we getting the hell out of here if it's so dangerous?"

"Look, cop—"

Paulo knew it was time to push Styx. "If I don't start hearing an explanation now, I'm calling my precinct."

"Try it," Styx told him through gritted teeth.

"Come on, Paulo. We'll figure it out," Law told him, and Paulo turned from Styx back to him. He was grateful Law was safe and in one piece, and wasn't ready to tell him about the photos in the assassin's pocket. Styx would have to let them both in on everything soon enough, and Law already looked wrecked.

"There's nothing to figure out—you'll listen to me and do what I say," Styx persisted, and Paulo didn't have to worry about punching the shit out of Styx, because Law was mad enough for both of them.

"What the hell are we supposed to do now? Hide out in some shithole until you catch whoever's shooting at us?" Law demanded, no doubt partly to distract him from the pissing contest he appeared to be in with Paulo.

Styx eyed him coolly. "Yes. Tell the cop to give me his phone. And then I'm taking both of you into protective custody."

Law shook his head. "You've got to be kidding me. What—now we're going into witness protection for reasons unknown? Bullshit."

"I know the reasons." Styx's eyes met Paulo's and the two men came to a silent agreement. "Like I said, I've been trying to avoid this for months."

"Why's it taken that long? Oh, wait, that's SOP for the CIA," Law muttered. "Who got killed here tonight?"

"You don't have the clearance for that intel," Styx told him, and Paulo watched the fireworks between these men with great interest. The tension there was extreme—sexual and otherwise, and Paulo couldn't believe he was stuck in the middle of them.

"So let me get this straight—the three of us have to hole up together so we don't get killed?" Paulo asked, and Styx nodded, looking as grim at that prospect as Paulo felt. "For how long?"

"As long as it takes."

"I am going to need way more of an explanation than that, Styx." Law ran a hand through his hair, his irritation mounting as evidenced by the tension in his shoulders. Paulo put a hand on one of them, because no matter what, Law was safe for now.

"We can't hang around here to discuss this," Styx told him. "I'll tell you more when we get someplace a little less public, all right?"

"You weren't worried about that earlier," Law growled, and Paulo made a mental note to find out what that was all about, but first he put his hand on Law's arm.

"There was an assassin I shot. He had pictures of us in his pocket," he told Law, who stared between him and Styx.

Paulo actually felt bad for the agent, because Styx looked at Law the way Paulo felt…and why would you stay away from someone you loved so damned much?

None of this made sense, but it appeared he'd have nothing but time on his hands to unravel it.

ALSO BY SE JAKES

Men of Honor Series
BOUND BY HONOR
BOUND BY LAW
TIES THAT BIND
BOUND BY DANGER
BOUND FOR KEEPS
BOUND TO BREAK

Phoenix, Inc. Series
NO BOUNDARIES

Inked Series
HOLD THE LINE
THIRDS

EE LTD. Universe
FREE FALLING

Hell or High Water Series
CATCH A GHOST
LONG TIME GONE
DAYLIGHT AGAIN
NOT FADE AWAY
IF I EVER *(forthcoming)*

Dirty Deeds Series
DIRTY DEEDS

Havoc MC Series
RUNNING WILD

Bluewater Bay (multi-author series)
NO EASY WAY (novella) in the *LIGHTS, CAMERA, ACTION* Anthology

WRITING AS STEPHANIE TYLER

Shelter Series
SHELTER ME
PIECES OF ME (coming Fall 2016)

Mirror Series
MIRROR ME
RULE OF THIRDS
WALK IN MY SHADOW
DOUBLE BLIND (coming 2017)

Skulls Creek MC Series
VIPERS RUN
VIPERS RULE

Section 8 Series
SURRENDER
UNBREAKABLE
FRAGMENTED

Defiance Series
DEFIANCE
REDEMPTION
SALVATION
TEMPERANCE

Dire Wolves Series
DIRE WARNING (prequel novella)
DIRE NEEDS
DIRE WANTS
DIRE DESIRES

Shadow Force Series
LIE WITH ME
PROMISES IN THE DARK
IN THE AIR TONIGHT
NIGHT MOVES
LONELY IS THE NIGHT

Hold Series
HARD TO HOLD
TOO HOT TO HOLD
HOLD ON TIGHT
HOLDING ON (novella)

Hot Nights, Dark Desires Anthology
NIGHT VISION (novella)

Harlequin Blaze
COMING UNDONE
RISKING IT ALL
BEYOND HIS CONTROL

WRITING AS SYDNEY CROFT

ACRO Series
RIDING THE STORM
UNLEASHING THE STORM
SEDUCED BY THE STORM
TAMING THE FIRE
TEMPTING THE FIRE
TAKEN BY FIRE
THREE THE HARD WAy (novella)

Hot Nights, Dark Desires Anthology
SHADOW PLAY (novella)

ABOUT THE AUTHOR

SE JAKES is the pen name for *New York Times* bestselling author Stephanie Tyler, and half the co-writing team of Sydney Croft. First published in 2011, SE Jakes has quickly risen to be a bestselling author in the LGBT romance genre, as well as a fan favorite. Her books are frequently highlighted in *USA Today* and have been reviewed by *Library Journal* and *RT Books Magazine*. She's been nominated by several sites for Favorite M/M author and has finaled in the Goodreads M/M Romance Readers Choice Awards in 7 categories. She's a hybrid author who writes for Riptide Publishing and Samhain Publishing, and she indie publishes as well.

STEPHANIE TYLER is the *New York Times* bestselling author of romance novels spanning multiple genres, including Romantic Suspense, New Adult, Paranormal Romance and Contemporary Romance. She's a hybrid author who writes for multiple publishers, including Random House, NAL/ Penguin, Harlequin, Carina Press, Mammoth Books, Belle Books and Samhain Publishing, as well as Riptide (as SE Jakes) and indie publishing. Her books have been translated into half a dozen languages, nominated for an RT Readers' Choice Award and garnered top picks from *RT Book Magazine* as well as starred reviews from *Publishers Weekly*. She's a frequent workshop presenter and has contributed stories for anthologies for charities, including **SEAL of My Dreams**, which has raised over 150K for the Veterans Medical Association.

SYDNEY CROFT is the alter ego of Stephanie Tyler and Larissa Ione, two *New York Times* bestselling authors who blend their very different writing interests into adventurous tales of erotic paranormal fiction. Together, they developed a world where people with extraordinary abilities, like the power to control storms, could live and work with others like them. The series has been described as "Erotica meets the X-Men," and is unique in its own "erotic superhero romance" niche. Larissa and Stephanie live in different states and communicate almost entirely through email, though they often get together for conferences and book signings.